CATALYSTS

BILL GAUTHIER

For Courtney Elizabeth.
Sometimes small things make the biggest impacts.

A lan Ashley looked at his hands. What good were they? What had he ever done with them? Type reports for things he couldn't care less about…. Pick his nose…. Eat. But what had they done?

The side of his face ached. He touched it. The indentations on the growing bump were more defined. What the hell was this?

It's me, the voice said.

At that moment, pain exploded from the large growth and Alan cried out. He slid off the couch, onto his knees, and wept.

"That's right," the voice said. "Let it out."

Alan stopped. The pain was still there, still ravaging, but he forgot about it. The voice hadn't sounded internal. It sounded like it was in the same room.

"You wanted me," the voice said. "And I've come."

Alan used the couch and the wobbly TV tray to stand. He stumbled, almost fell, but finally stood. His legs quivered and he didn't know if he could walk, but knew he had to try. He had to get to the mirror. He made his way down the small hallway to the bathroom and flicked the switch. That explosion of pain had been the growth opening up. Two new eyes looked at him. A new nose breathed and a new mouth smiled.

"You created me," the face said. "You wanted me long enough and then you try to destroy me. That's fine. I'll just do what you never could because you were too weak."

CONTENTS

ACKNOWLEDGMENTS

FROM THE 2007 EDITION

These stories were written between 1998 and 2005. A lot happened in that time and while I can take credit for most of what's offered to you, I should really share some of it. The following people have helped me, these stories, this book, and my writing in some way or another during these years (and in a few cases, for longer). If you don't see your name here and think it should be, then I either forgot (in which case I'm sorry) or I don't want to list you (in which case you can go wallow). And I'm asshole enough to let you decide which category you fall into. So, thanks go to:

Donna Taylor Burgess, Kurt Charbonneau and family, Chris Clarke, Cathy Freeze, Kim Gatesman, Tracy Gauthier, Greg F. Gifune (big time, man!), Toby and Leslie Gray (and thank you both again for everything else!), Nicole Guerra, Everett Hoagland, Maureen Lacasse, Laura Stout LaTour, Michelle Marshall, Tom and Elizabeth Monteleone, B.J. Nooth, Aaron Pickering, Jorj Pitter, and Amber Pombo.

I want to thank James Beach for having the faith in my abilities to go ahead with this project.

I need to thank Mom and Dad—Pat and Ray Gauthier—for their support.

I want to thank my daughter, Courtney Elizabeth, for being a constant muse.

And lastly, I want to thank Kelly. While things didn't work out, she supported me more than she should have and encouraged me when no one else did. *Thank you.*

FOR THE 2021 EDITION

A quick thanks are due to Michelle Alexander, Mike de Gouveia, and Denise Angelo and Dan DeAraujo for the continued encouragement.

BIG thanks to rock 'n roll star Red Reveal himself, Randy Medeiros, for being so eager to read the Next Thing. Go buy his albums under Red Reveal. If you like Metallica and Van Halen and good ol' rock 'n roll, this guy's got the goods!

Thanks to David Niall Wilson and David Dodd at Crossroad Press and Macabre Ink for bringing my babies back.

My mother died in February 2019, and I hope she knew how much her support meant to me, and I'm terribly sad that she can't see this new edition. My father now is the cheerleader and while I know he won't read this, I'll let him know I mention him.

Thanks to my younger daughter, Genevieve, who often clicks the *Submit* button for me before submitting work and for being proud of her old man.

Again, to my daughter Courtney, who is an adult now. Hard work pays off, kiddo.

And lastly, my wife Pamela, who puts up with my shit but doesn't take it. She constantly encourages me to keep pushing and submitting. She's my biggest cheerleader and proves that happiness makes people more creative than unhappiness. Love you, Blueberry Muffin.

ECHOES ON THE POND

(coming Spring 2023)

When thirteen-year-old Missy Walters goes to child counselor Cheryl Turcotte under court order, their combined troubled pasts raise a deadly ghost from her watery grave. The ghost wishes to return to life by possessing Missy. Now Missy and Cheryl must face their pasts and fix their present in order to stop the ghost from making Missy disappear forever.

Missy is new to the Boston neighborhood of Jamaica Plain. She got in trouble, again, and now lives with her father, Blake, after the court granted him custody. Part of Missy's continued freedom hinges on her undergoing counseling to deal with dark secrets from her past. Her new counselor, Cheryl, also has dark secrets from her past. She and her younger sister, Kristen, were terribly abused by their mother, who Cheryl killed in self-defense when she was seventeen. When the ghost of a teenage girl begins haunting them, their lives descend into a hell of self-doubt, fear, and violence. In order to defeat the evil spirit, Missy and Cheryl must find out who the girl is, why she haunts them, and how to move beyond their own tragic pasts to save themselves and their loved ones.

SHADOWED

From the corner of her eye, she sees him: A shadow-man frenetically moving, reaching out for her, yearning. Fear grips Gina Copeland. Her life has been turned upside down by her parents' recent divorce and a move from her childhood home. Her friends have grown more distant as new friends and interests have come into their lives.

The Shadow-Man can't be real. Can he?

She feels his yearning. His touch mesmerizes. Gina's loneliness evaporates as she falls into an ethereal seduction that she knows is wrong yet cannot resist. But what's the worst that can happen? She's about to find out as she struggles to stop everything she loves from slipping away.

ALICE ON THE SHELF

Where's Alice?

Down the Rabbit Hole.When Brad awakens with this question on his lips but his friend Miranda on his mind, a sense of unease fills him. When he finds she isn't home, and a strange visitor is outside her house looking for a missing pocket watch, Brad knows something is amiss. The world is familiar but different. Storybooks, fairy tales, nursery rhymes, and fantasies should have prepared Brad for the trip he is about to embark on to find the woman he loves, but the darkness that has filled this fantastic world has twisted it almost beyond recognition.Though he is searching for his friend, Brad may discover something much darker when he finds -

Alice On The Shelf

GHOSTS OF A CATALYST

THE 2021 INTRODUCTION

Who the hell does this guy think he is to make us suffer through two *introductions?!* That's what the reptilian spot in my brain is expecting you to be thinking. Let me explain, if you will. If you prefer not to go through my two introductions, feel free to skip ahead to the first story, the one I may be best known for, "The Growth of Alan Ashley." But if you're like me and enjoy the introductions in collections, then stick around. I'll try to make it worth your while.

First off, I don't entirely *love* the 2007 introduction. I mean, it's all right, but there's this feeling of a bright-eyed kid that's not entirely right. I was excited to be *asked* to do a collection, and it felt like I was at the start of a very special road. And I was, but not in the way I thought. The two years between when James R. Beach pitched the idea until its eventual publication saw tons of change. In the nearly fourteen years since publication, even more has changed.

Catalysts came out as Dark Discoveries Publications first—and really only—book. Soon after publication, *Dark Discoveries*, the magazine that spawned the book line and for which I was writing my column, *American Gauthic*, went through changes as a new co-publisher/editor came in. I wasn't fond of the changes he brought with him. James was a great guy, but the direction the new version of *Dark Discoveries* was going seemed counterproductive. Instead of discovering new talents, it looked backward to icons of the horror/dark fantastic genre. There's certainly an importance in looking back at those masters who've come before, but the focus, which was more than coincidental and I wonder if it was anything other than self-serving to the new editor/publisher, should've been on *discovering* new writers. Eventually, I got tired of barbs being edited into my essays by the new editor/publisher that I would have to then edit out because I won't let passive-aggressive bullshit be woven into my work. He was the kind of guy that when he eventually decided to leave the magazine, right before it was sold, he emailed me to try out his new magazine while also insulting James.

The other major reason I stopped writing *American Gauthic* was that I got tired of having to chase down payment for my work. It wasn't a lot of bread, but it was bread. Eventually, I just stopped writing the column and the magazine limped along until it was eventually sold to Journalstone and found a new life. I will always value the chances James gave me. This book wouldn't exist without him.

It did all right, I'm told, but eventually it didn't, and that was my fault. I knew nothing about self-promotion. I was a stunted thirty-year-old who thought people would come to me, asking for interviews, etc. Looking back, I'm embarrassed. And even then, going into my other books a few years later, *Alice on the Shelf* and *Shadowed*, the same thing happened. I ended up buying the rest of the *Catalysts* stock and still have copies. Looking back, there's a lot I would change.

As far as the stories go, I think some of them are pretty good for a guy who was in his twenties when they were written. Some, I'm not sure about. "Inquisitor, Inc.," for instance, is a story I've grown uncomfortable with, as it smacks of misogyny. It came from a nightmare I had and I'd been told that it wasn't misogynistic, but…. I almost pulled it from this edition, but I think the ending clarifies that the story does not support the actions of the main character, and there isn't any glorification of the terrible things that happen to the poor woman in the story. Still, I don't know that time has been kind to it.

I also decided to add a story called "KILL -13-", which was published the year after *Catalysts* originally came out. It's the only story in this collection written after 2005 (and when I was already in my thirties!). It fits into this collection quite well, I think. It's a story that's scary more because of the subject matter—school shootings and crazy people with easy access to guns—than from any ghosts or monsters.

Some of the stories that I remembered fondly felt a little clunky when I revised them for this edition (I'm hoping I've smoothed them out a little), while some that I had considered "minor" are actually quite enjoyable. It was a pleasant experience going back to these stories.

In the years since *Catalysts* went out of print, a lot has happened. I remarried and have another daughter. I spent a *long* time writing a novel that, as of this writing, I'm marketing. It actually features characters from two different stories in this book. I won't say which two, though, that way whenever it finds a home and finds its way into your hands you'll be surprised, but it was interesting to take two characters from two different stories and put them together in a new, *very* different novel.

In the end, the reason I even wanted *Catalysts* back out there (besides ego, har har) was that I really like the stories. The collection was a start of something for me, and I still love it. I'm happy that you'll get to read the tales within. Just be careful, some of them may unsettle you.

Bill Gauthier
Dartmouth, Massachusetts
March 12th, 2021

THE CATALYST: BEGINNING THE DREAM

THE ORIGINAL 2007 INTRODUCTION

What you're holding in your hands is part of a dream. While the dream's roots go back to my early childhood, it officially took form on 24 August 1990, the day I turned thirteen.

I'd just come home with *The Shining*. I didn't really read much but I had a strange curiosity about it. I'd chosen to read *The Shining* because 1) I loved horror movies and knew the name Stephen King from them, 2) I'd seen an interview with Stephen King on a nightly news magazine the night before, and 3) I figured if I didn't finish the book, I could watch the movie. It took me three or four months, but I indeed finished the book. One of the most important moments of my life happened at the beginning of the novel, when Jack Torrance is being shown the basement. I had a sort of out-of-body experience. I was *interested* in a basement of an old hotel. Nothing had happened yet (except for Torrance thinking of Ullman as an *officious little prick*) and I was still hooked. Somehow, I realized that this man's writing, his *storytelling*, had hooked me and, in a fit of youthful hubris, I decided it was something that I could do.

Within days, I'd set up a couple of milk crates and began pounding—with one finger—on a Royal Quiet De Luxe manual typewriter.

I've written about that *ad nauseum* and for those who have read it already, I apologize for repeating myself (although I'm sure there are many around me who have had to sit through me telling that story *many* times and will no doubt hear it many more, so consider yourself lucky), but I felt it was needed here, too.

If we're going to start something (and that's the point of any catalyst, isn't it?), then we should start at the beginning. I began writing at that moment.

Maybe it was still having the interview (which aired on *Primetime Live*), which had a shot of King sitting at a typewriter clacking away, fresh in my mind. Or maybe it was because the back of the book said King lived in Maine. Being from Massachusetts, the idea of making movies—another passion of mine—seemed too far away (now it doesn't, what with digital technology) so I never really gave much credence to doing what another hero, George Lucas, has been able to do. Whatever the reason, writing took hold of me and I focused on becoming the best writer I was capable of becoming.

Of course, I'm still on that quest. I still aim to become the best writer I can.

I've always loved stories. My earliest memories are of me lying on the old, green couch straight out of the 1970s, my head resting on Mom's lap, sucking on a baw-baw, while she read to me. I remember watching TV. Not just cartoons or kids shows (not that there were many kids shows in those days before 24-hour cable channels that catered to children) but Mom's soap operas (I remember Luke and Laura getting married), sitcoms (*Happy Days* and *Mork & Mindy* were favorites), dramas (*The Incredible Hulk* and *CHiPs*), and the movie of the week. There were more, too, no doubt. On his way home from work, Dad would often bring home comic books. I loved my three-to-four-inch action figures, particularly after I discovered *Star Wars* in a 1982 rerelease. I also had Underoos in which I could dress up as Batman, Superman, or Spider-Man; cut-off jeans and no shirt or shoes allowed me to become the Hulk. A stick and toy gun allowed me to be Luke Skywalker.

When I played, though, I didn't just play. I told (or acted out) stories. Somehow, my mother was able to pass along the idea that the stories I knew were made up by people. That George Lucas was responsible for the delights I knew onscreen from that galaxy far, far away. That Superman didn't really fly, sometimes he was on wires and sometimes on a table. She wasn't a

Grinch, mind you, trying to take the magic out of things, she was a parent of a child with a *very* active imagination who might try jumping out the window once his red cape was tied on. By knowing that people had made that stuff up, she stopped certain disasters.

And maybe even caused a few.

Because, as Harlan Ellison has said, "success is achieving in adult terms that which you desired as a child." I haven't achieved that success yet. But I'm working on it. This book is a step on that path.

When I sit down to write a first draft of something, I'm playing with my action figures. It's me and the story and fuck anyone else. If *I'm* happy, then that's all that matters. Once the first draft is done and has been allowed to rest a bit, I go back and read it and edit it with my blue pen. At this point, I'm still thinking about my likes and dislikes, but I've begun to think about others, too. What will a reader, my ideal reader, think? What about friends? Will this entertain them? And how's the writing? Mark Twain said, "The difference between the right word and the almost right word is the difference between lightning and the lightning bug." Do I have a lightning bug on my hands or a bolt of lightning that'll fry your ass?

Once the editing is done (this usually takes more time than it should because it's the most like work, and yet, I still love doing it), I sit at the computer and revise it. Once that's done, I let people read it. I have a few friends that I can trust to give me honest feedback. They tell me what they think and then I edit and revise for a third draft. And then I begin submitting.

Afterward, I may edit and revise more. As is the case with most of the stories in *Catalysts*.

Mere days before my twenty-eighth birthday in 2005, James Beach called me. I had just sat in bed to begin reading the advance copy of Neil Gaiman's novel *Anansi Boys* when the phone rang. I almost didn't answer it because I didn't recognize the phone number. James and I had worked together for more than a year. I've had work in every issue of his magazine

Dark Discoveries. The first two issues featured my stories "The Umbrella People" and "Fun Gus the Tap Dance Man." The third issue premiered my column *American Gauthic.* We talked about three hours on a range of topics. Somewhere during the chatting, he proposed the idea of collecting some of my stories for the first book project from Dark Discoveries Publications. He'd taken a chance on my column and now he wanted to take a chance on a book. And my mother used to call *me* a glutton for punishment.

After we talked, a verbal handshake was made and I began work on getting the stories together and rewriting and revising them.

Each of these stories has acted as a catalyst, often allowing me to write whatever story followed them at the time. In the case of "The Growth of Alan Ashley," working on the story not only made it possible to write the stories I wrote afterward, but its publication (and subsequent reprints) acted as a catalyst to my career. And since this is my first book….

So here we are, experiencing together a little bit of a dream. I hope you have as much fun reading these stories as I had writing them. I also hope that we'll be able to sit together again. Because I have more stories that I'd like to tell you. And other dreams I'd like to share.

Bill Gauthier
New Bedford, Massachusetts
5 March 2006

THE GROWTH OF ALAN ASHLEY

At five-thirty, his alarm clock's radio came on and the radio personality spoke to a caller about world affairs. Alan Ashley's eyes popped open. What day was it? Wednesday. The interview! The morning show began at seven. His segment was supposed to be at 7:30, right after they came back from commercial and local news. Alan's new book had just been released and was already predicted to be the rage this season, every bit as popular as his movie this past summer. He looked forward to speaking with the morning show anchor again.

Alan noticed the growth near his right ear while shaving. A smooth bump that resembled a blister but would not pop. Probably an ingrown hair. He ignored it, finished getting ready, and left the apartment.

He drove himself to the studio where the morning show was aired. Traffic was bad and he was afraid he'd be late. Alan entered the building and went to the elevator. He blocked out everything around him, though. The morning show was done at ground level so the crowds outside could watch. The elevator stopped on the fourth floor and Alan stepped out.

"We need that report by eleven, Alan," the producer said, too busy to stop and formally greet him.

Report. Must've been talking to the newswoman before Alan arrived and had mixed up *report* with *autographed books.*

Alan sighed and walked toward the green room. It was rather small, considering how popular the morning show was and how many guests were usually on, but Alan didn't complain. He plopped his briefcase down

(When had he picked it up?)

It has a new manuscript for your editor in it.

(Yeah, that's good.)

and flicked awake the computer. He looked over the walls of the cubicle—*green room*, he corrected himself—and saw no one. His watch said 7:30 and he sat.

The morning show anchor waited for the signal and began with the intro. A few seconds later, Alan was on, chatting with the anchor. It was amazing that this book, just like his last one, was selling off the shelves. How could he explain it?

"I can't," Alan said, looking at his shoes, fashionably modest. "I just write the best story I can."

The anchor smiled, amazed, and asked about whether the success of the latest movie might have had an influence.

"It's possible, I guess," said Alan. "The thing is, though, I don't really notice. It's as though I'm two people sometimes. One worries about the movies, one about the books."

The morning show anchor reminded Alan that he'd also acted and produced, as well as directed the movie.

"I guess, then, there's more than two—" Alan began to say when movement out of the corner of his eye made him turn.

Gina stood at the opening of the cubicle, a tote bag dangling from her shoulder, her jacket still on. Her eyes were wide as she stared at Alan, a bemused smile on her face.

"Good morning, Alan," she said, looking around the cubicle. "Who're you talking to?"

His right leg, which had been resting on his left knee, dropped. The bump near his ear itched and Alan scratched at it, his face heating up. He looked at the clock in the corner of his computer monitor. 7:37 AM. He'd expected Roland—the producer—to be here, but no one else usually got here until closer to eight. Especially Gina, who had the cubicle beside his. She continued staring at him, expectantly.

"I was thinking aloud," he said.

Her stare didn't falter. Neither did the bemused smiled. "About movies and books?"

"Yes."

"And you write what you can?" The bemusement bordered on taunting.

It felt as though his heart, stomach, testicles—everything—turned to concrete and fell.

"It looked like you were...talking to someone," she said. The familiar smile, like from when he was in school. "Like you were being...*interviewed*."

Alan was on his feet before he realized he was going to stand, and he reached out, hands trembling.

"*Please*," he whispered, face on fire. "*Please* don't say anything to anyone. Sometimes I—I—"

Gina shook her head and stepped toward her cubicle. The smile was gone, replaced with something else. "Calm down, Alan. I won't say anything."

"My career, my life, would be ruined. Please—"

"I said I wouldn't say anything. I won't."

She disappeared behind a cubicle partition. Alan thought about following her, making sure she wouldn't say anything to anyone, but didn't. Instead, he sat and his thumb went to his mouth to be gnawed.

It was bound to have happened sooner or later. Reality, like a giant monster from an old Japanese monster movie, destroys everything at some point. He'd had to hide these lives for twenty years, since the kids in seventh grade began making fun of him for acting out his stories outside. Something he'd spent his life doing all of a sudden taken from him.

No! a voice in his head demanded. *Stay focused. Roland wants that report by eleven, do it by ten. Go out for lunch. You have a meeting with Scorsese about his new movie.*

Alan tried to push the voice away as he wheeled his chair closer to the computer. He realized his wet, bleeding thumb was no longer in his mouth, but near his ear. His hand rubbed at the growth. He made a mental note to keep an eye on it.

Though the lunch meeting with Scorsese went very well (the great director wanted *Alan* to play a hitman in his next movie... time permitting, of course) Alan's heart sank as he walked past Gina's cubicle. He stopped and stepped back, looking in. The photographs, art magazine clippings, all personal effects were gone. The back of his neck prickled with the feeling of eyes on him. Alan turned. He barely glimpsed Gina and Francine's heads disappearing behind a partition several cubicles away.

Then came the sound of laughter trying to be suppressed.

Alan's eyes went to the floor and he went back to his cubicle. He spent the rest of the afternoon trying to work, though he swore he could feel the eyes of many people looking at him. A disturbance in the Force, perhaps.

Your adoring fans, the voice reassured him.

Alan watched Jimmy Fallon and Seth Myers. Then he went back and watched Jimmy Kimmel and James Corden. Of course, he watched Stephen Colbert and Trevor Noah. Lying in bed after the shows, listening to a podcast interview with Paul Rudd, he watched light travel across his ceiling from cars speeding up and down the street. The thing near his ear had gone from itching to burning, but not too badly. It was there but he was becoming used to it.

The voices from the radio alarm clock didn't penetrate Alan's mind, not this night. He remembered the look Gina had given him. That smile—no, *smirk*. He remembered that smirk. He'd seen it in school as a boy and then as a teenager. That smirk that people gave to someone who was strange to them, outside their narrow view of the world and how it should be, some-one who didn't fit the "typical" mold, the Phantom of the Opera or Quasimodo or even Carrie White. He swore he'd never see that look again. Yet, here he was, fifteen years after high school, eleven after college, having been looked at like that again. The shell that had been so carefully built around him, that had protected him those long study hall periods and gym classes, that had comforted him after girlfriends had found the note-book with the movie lists and poster designs that he'd made and noticed the dates, that shell with its intricate ornamentation had been removed years ago. He'd realized he'd never meet a woman with his kind of imagination. Never. They'd never truly understand him. That was fine, he could live with that. But now, when he was supposed to be safe, supposed to be okay with himself, that goddamn motherfucking *look*.

Alan sat, tossing his legs off the side of the bed. The growth felt bigger to him but he ignored it as his overactive imagina-tion, hypochondria. It works both ways, imagination does. The thing that produces great Art—films, music, literature, paintings, sculptures, and so much more—is also the genesis of fears, anxieties, paranoia.

The radio personality asked him about the rumors of the new Scorsese movie on the heels of the novel's selling more copies than anyone ever had in one week. Alan opened his mouth, ready to answer and stopped. This wasn't right. For Christ's sake, it wasn't right. He was thirty-two years old and should *know* better. It was purer if he kept the fantasies separate. A movie actor/writer/producer/director, that was fine. A novelist/screenwriter/and sometimes-maybe-if-they-let-me director was fine. But not together. Sure, there were those people who lived those lives, but it was better to separate them.

The growth near his ear burned and itched but it faded as Alan Ashley, novelist, chatted about his new novel. He *was* on a book tour, after all.

Thursday and Friday passed. Both days were hell for Alan. He went to work early, just as he always did, and felt the change in the office as Thursday progressed. There were whispers. People seemed to pass by his cubicle more often than normal, peeking in as they went like people new to cubicle work often did. The voice in his head told him it was because they'd heard his radio interview this morning on their way to work but Alan tried to ignore the voice. Also, the growth *was* larger.

More of the same on Friday. Alan hoped the weekend would quiet the whispers down. Maybe being away for two days, getting on with their lives, they'd forget about what Gina had seen and reported.

Gina. That lying bitch. She said she wouldn't say anything. That fucking lying cunt. He had the mind to—

To what? the voice asked. *You want to go down in history like Fatty Arbuckle, O.J. Simpson, and Phil Spector?*

Alan calmed himself.

Throughout Friday, it felt as though the growth were on fire. The pain pulsating from it seemed to send a high-pitch buzzing through Alan's head until his brain ached. The afternoon was a waste. Nothing got done. He touched the mouse slightly every time the screensaver came up, but never actually did anything. No reports were written, nothing was analyzed. Yet, he forced himself to stay later than everyone else so he wouldn't have to go through the nightmare he'd gone through Thursday, of standing in an elevator with his coworkers as they smirked, stealing glances at him through the corner of their eyes.

He got home Friday night and crashed on the couch. He watched the *E! True Hollywood Story* marathon. Maybe it was time to end the fantasies. Maybe it was time to grow up and stop living false lives, begin living a real one.

But how do you want to go out? the voice in his head asked. *Who does what?*

The musician was mostly dormant unless a really good song came on the radio, so he would be easy. The writer would be tough right now and so would the actor/producer/director.

Alan threw on some music and rocked to Bruce Springsteen, Aerosmith, Metallica, Billy Joel, and Elton John. He ended with Springsteen four hours later and, covered in sweat, waved to the audience. By the time he got to the limo, reviewers were hailing this first concert of the tour the best concert he'd ever given. He played and performed as though there were no tomorrow. One reviewer even wrote that they didn't know how he'd be able to make a whole tour with that kind of energy. However, Alan the musician wouldn't need to worry. His private plane went down in Idaho. The famous rock 'n roll musician, Alan Ashley, was dead at thirty-two.

The writer, cliché or not, took to drinking. There was no booze in Alan's apartment, he couldn't hold it, but there was plenty of Diet Pepsi. At a benefit, Alan drank. He was supposed to speak that night and he went to the podium. The growth's burning, itching, humming, was almost too much to handle and Alan suspected he felt like he was really drunk.

"Thank you for inviting me to speak to you this evening," Alan said, trying hard not to slur his words but knowing they would still come out that way. "I just got word, tonight, that my book has sold more copies in such a short period of time

20

BILL GAUTHIER

than any other book by any other author. Maybe I celebrated too early. Fukkit."

Alan went on for almost two hours. He babbled about the life he'd created for this fantasy, how he'd run with street gangs and had gotten secret access to all sorts of lifestyles. He talked about the art of writing and the commerce of publishing. He went on until he finally passed out.

Alan lay on the worn carpet, the growth pointing toward the ceiling. It ached. Throbbed. Sent out waves of sound through his head. He pushed himself off the floor, went to the bathroom, and looked in the mirror, staying in character. How had he gotten to his hotel room? What had he said that night?

The growth was bigger. It was no longer smooth but had indentations.

I'm going to have to have that checked out, Alan thought.

You're out of character, the voice in his head told him.

"Fuck you," Alan mumbled. "This is serious."

But he slipped back into the problems of the alcoholic writer. No, not alcoholic. He'd gone on for years saying he didn't drink. He couldn't rewrite that history, could he? All those awards he'd received from MADD and SADD and other organizations for being a good role model. Then what? A one-night binge. His first. Only on an extremely bad night.

Alan went to bed. He didn't watch any interview shows. He allowed sleep to take him even though they needed to travel over the painful road the growth was paving.

He awoke to excruciating pain that tore through his head and brought tears to his eyes. In the bathroom he flicked the switch and stared into the mirror. The bump had grown more overnight. The side of his face now looked swollen. Gravity seemed to dissipate. He stared at his new visage, unaware of the physical world around him, his ramming heart the only sound in the world. He needed to get to the emergency room, *now.*

You're fine, the voice in his head said. *It'll go away by Monday. Just give it some time.*

Alan couldn't take his eyes off it. The growth almost took up the whole side of his face. How could he not go to the hospital?

The papers, the voice said. *You made the papers.*

They reported Alan Ashley, best-selling author of numerous novels and stories, had ruined his image by being drunk at a benefit. It wasn't the drunkenness the socialites didn't like, either. Fuck, most of *them* had been drunk. It was the fact he had denounced so many of them for drinking and then had gone up on stage drunk. He ruined the evening when he passed out and fell on the table of *the Vice President of the United States.* The TV reported the event, noting that sales of his books were already dipping and half the bookstores in the country weren't even open yet. His agent called and told him that Oprah didn't want him on her show now after all. He called back half an hour later to report that his publisher was dropping him because he'd groped the head honcho's wife.

Shattered by his own momentary stupidity, his weakness, he went into his bedroom and opened a desk drawer. The gun was in the back, just as it had always been. He took it out, looked at it. Then he put it in his mouth and closed his eyes. If it had been good enough for Hemingway....

He squeezed the trigger.

Alan fell back on the bed at the sound of the dry click of plastic on plastic. He lay there, staring at the ceiling, writing the obituary of Alan Ashley, author. He took his own life in the Plaza Hotel in New York. He didn't even write a final note.

After an hour of lying on the bed with the growth throbbing, Alan sat up. The toy gun was still in his hand. He remembered playing cops and robbers with it as a boy. Until he couldn't anymore. Until he'd been harassed for his need to act things out.

The actor, the voice said. *One last time.*

It was a party in L.A. Alan Ashley, who began acting in his teens and had become a screenwriter, producer, and director, wasn't usually found on the party scene. But a mid-morning party couldn't lead to trouble, could it? This was L.A., though. He was with the cream of the crop—this year's Brat Pack, last year's Brat Pack, fuck, the *original* Brat Pack. In the kitchen, Alan Ashley, who'd won awards for being a good role model to kids by not doing drugs or even drinking, decided to give in a little.

He tried a drink. Then he snorted some coke. He loved it. By the end of Saturday, he was on a binge. Everyone told him to slow down. You're gonna end up like John Belushi, they told him. Or River Pheonix or Chris Farley or Philip Seymour Hoffman or.....

But he didn't stop. He stayed up Saturday night doing lines and drinking and floating in the cloud that seemed to come from the growth on his face. It still ached and throbbed. He paid it no mind. In the early-morning hours of Sunday, Alan Ashley, famed actor, died of a drug overdose. His agent found him in his Malibu home.

Alan Ashley, who'd been born, raised, and lived in Harden, Massachusetts, sat on his couch and stared at the blank TV. On the TV tray in front of him was the paper plate he'd used to snort the flour, a rolled-up one dollar bill lying near it. Empty Diet Pepsi cans littered the apartment. The walls were bare. No artwork, no photographs, nothing. Books, videos, and DVDs and Blu-rays were stacked around the place. His clothes lay strewn about. The apartment cost twelve hundred dollars a month. He had trouble paying it. His freezer in the kitchen consisted mainly of frozen entrees. The refrigerator was almost empty except for milk and soda. He owned only a few dishes, hand-me-downs from his parents. The semen stains in his sheets were not from the different women he met on book signings or press junkets, not actresses or fans, but from himself, by himself.

Alan Ashley, a marketing guy for a firm in Harden. He went to work daily, sat in front of the computer or on the phone analyzing sales and marketing, not really important, not making waves. Usually his coworkers nodded to him, aware of his existence but unaware of *him*, the person. Gina being the only one because she'd had the cubicle near his. Now they were aware of him, but for what? For talking to himself. For living in fantasies.

Alan Ashley looked at his hands. What good were they? What had he ever done with them? Type reports for things he couldn't care less about. Jerk off. Pick his nose. Wipe his ass. Eat. But what had they *done*?

The side of his face ached. He touched it. The indentations on the growing bump were more defined. What the hell was this?

It's me, the voice said.

At that moment, pain exploded from the large growth and Alan cried out. He slid off the couch, onto his knees, and wept.

"That's right," the voice said. "Let it out."

Alan stopped. The pain was still there, still ravaging, but he forgot about it. The voice hadn't sounded internal. It sounded like it was in the same room.

"You wanted me," the voice said. "And I've come."

Alan used the couch and the wobbly TV tray to stand. He stumbled, almost fell, but finally stood. His legs quivered and he didn't know if he could walk, but knew he had to try. He had to get to the mirror. He made his way down the small hallway to the bathroom and flicked the switch. That explosion of pain had been the growth opening up. Two new eyes looked at him. A new nose breathed and a new mouth smiled.

"You created me," the face said. "You wanted me long enough and then you try to destroy me. That's fine. I'll just do what you never could because *you* were too weak."

Alan screamed while the face that had grown beside his laughed. When the screams died, Alan realized he couldn't feel his body. That sensation of zero-g had returned. Only now, when he tried to raise his hand to touch the growth, it wouldn't move. When he wanted to run from the bathroom, his feet wouldn't respond.

Alan watched as Sunday became Monday and he quit his job, telling Roland to take his reports and stuff 'em. He watched as he told Gina that she was a lying, backstabbing cunt and should go home and take the bottle of antidepressants the same way her mother had. He watched, though through a fog, as Tuesday came and he packed a few books, DVDs and Blu-rays, and CDs with his clothes. As he took the money out of the bank. As he got in his car and began driving.

Somewhere in Pennsylvania, heading west, Alan saw himself as a growth that was fading on a face. This face knew what it wanted, knew what it would do. Alan watched as the hand that had once been his came up and its fingernail dug into him. He was aware of being pulled off, pain tearing through him, until everything went black.

DRAWN IN

It was a perfectly good mattress, except that it was made for a toddler's bed. That and it also had a large, inverted-pyramid-shaped indentation in its very center. Harry didn't know *how* the indentation got there, nor did he care. What he knew (and cared about) was that the other side of the mattress was flat and would be better than sleeping on flattened cardboard boxes.

Under the bridge and behind some bushes, in an area he thought of as His Spot, Harry sat on the newfound mattress with the copy of *The Grapes of Wrath* he'd borrowed from the library and wondered how the others were faring in the shelters tonight. Once spring came, unless there was a really bad storm or the humidity became unbearable, Harry stayed away from the shelters. The cheap watch he'd found this past Christmas said it was around eight-thirty when Harry gave in and began eating the tuna fish sandwich he'd been saving. He looked across the river at the docks on the Fairview side.

The sandwich was soon gone and Harry wiped the crumbs from his beard. Voices came from nearby and he froze, holding his breath. His ears perked and tried to hear every sound around him. The voices grew closer until Harry expected some young punks to come through the bushes, but then they faded away. He let out a breath he hardly knew he'd held. This nook in the city of Harden was mainly unknown. Cars passed overhead and occasional litter fell from the bridge but Harry was pretty much left alone to watch the fishing boats or the gulls ride the current, or the docked boats and the beaches across the river.

Time passed and Harry's eyes grew heavy. He'd thought about the family he'd not seen in years but tonight the memories were sweeter than usual, without the bitterness or sorrow (god*damn* the sorrow) or anger that interweaved them. His eyes closed and before sleep engulfed him, he thought that it was very nice indeed to have found such a nice mattress abandoned like that.

Something poked up through the mattress into his back. Along with that discomfort, cold wind blew through his thin hair and penetrated the shield of his beard, chilling him. Harry hugged himself and reached for the blanket, but felt nothing but the bare mattress. Eyes still closed, not wanting to fully wake up, he reached off the mattress and hoped that the blanket was within reach but his fingers touched nothing. No blanket, no *ground*.

Harry's eyes opened. His heart rocketed into his throat and cut off his breath. The ground wasn't there. The bridge that connected Harden to Fairview and everything around it was gone. Even the night sky had been replaced by a multicolored sunrise or sunset.

Harry screamed and his voice echoed below him. He turned and the mattress rocked. He grabbed hold of it, though he didn't know why. The mattress teetered atop a mountain summit; the kind of mountain summit seen in cartoons and children's drawings. His own daughter, Mindy, had drawn mountains like this. As a matter of fact, hadn't one drawing been—?

Something cawed over him and blotted out the sun. An eagle with a wingspan roughly the size of a jetliner's soared around the mountaintop. It rose vertically, then turned and dove. A scream began in the pit of Harry's stomach as the enormous eagle plunged for him and the scream rolled up and up and finally burst from his mouth and—

He awoke. The blankets lay in a heap on the ground. The moon had disappeared and the bridge's traffic had become a trickle. Across the river, most of the buildings and houses had darkened; only a few businesses' security lights and streetlamps lit the coast.

Harry sat up, grabbed his warm Pepsi, and took a swig. His hands trembled and heart raced.

Calm down, he told himself. *It was only a dream.*

But it had felt so real. Even now, the cool spring night felt warmer than the dream's cold mountain air.

Harry stood and lifted the mattress. Just as he thought, he hadn't missed any large rocks when he'd laid the mattress down. There was only that strange indentation, which probably explained the source of the nightmare. The mattress plopped down, kicking up dust and dry, brown leaves.

He lay down. Only a few years ago, Harry probably wouldn't have been able to sleep again tonight. Ignoring his mind's unwelcome replay of time's passage, he wrapped himself in the blankets.

No matter how hard Harry tried to ignore reminders of the past, the mountains that had adorned Mindy's early drawings seeped into his mind. He remembered her as a young child, before his anger had taken over his soul, before booze had taken over his life. She'd spent hours drawing. She'd been fascinated by the obvious differences and hidden similarities between city and country and had drawn rickety cityscapes juxtaposed against jagged countryside. Mountains were prominent in many of her country pieces, especially after they'd driven through New Hampshire's White Mountains on vacation. In Southeastern Massachusetts, there were no mountains. Beaches, yes. Woods, yes. Fields, yes. Mountains, no. And, like so many children before her, her mountain ranges resembled inverted V's. At some point, fantastic creatures began cropping up both in the city- and landscapes. By then, though, Harry had begun living in his own darkly fantastic world.

Tears filled his eyes. He'd seen Mindy two weeks ago.

Almost hadn't recognized her. Mindy's hair had been cut to shoulder length and she...well, she'd become a woman. They'd made eye contact. He'd wanted to speak to her but turned and walked away instead. What would he have said? He'd been homeless for fifteen years, out on the street by her tenth birthday. Sure, he'd been sober seven years now but that didn't change the past. He knew she'd become a successful artist and lived an hour away in Boston. That was good; at least he'd never held her back.

He'd never held her back.

With that thought in mind, Harry fell once again into sleep's velvet cloak.

KAW!

Harry's eyes opened to a clear blue sky instead of the underside of the bridge. He grasped to the sides of the mattress. The enormous eagle once again circled above.

Have to wake up, he thought. *Have to get outta this goddamn dream!*

Except he couldn't force himself to wake up this time. Wind gusted into the mountain and the wobbling mattress. Harry's grasp tightened. Why the hell did he keep dreaming about this goddamn place?

The eagle swept down and clutched Harry in its oversized talons. Harry screamed as the bird carried him away from the swaying mattress before it plummeted from the mountaintop, occasionally bouncing off the mountain until it disappeared into a sea of pastel clouds.

Harry's eyes watered as the enormous eagle carried him through the clouds. As they descended, a vegetation-blanketed world lay below. Fields of lush swaying grasses spotted a forest that went off in all directions until jagged mountain ranges stopped them. In the far distance, a cityscape the likes of which he'd never seen rose, somehow a natural outcrop of the surrounding countryside. The eagle cawed and dove. Harry might've screamed had his jaw unclenched. He gripped the talons until his hands ached.

The eagle glided down toward a field until it was within several feet of the grass, then dropped him. He hit the thick grass softly and rolled a few feet while the eagle gave a final caw and flew away.

When Harry got up, his dirty, old, and wrinkled clothes were replaced by simple jeans and a chambray shirt with the sleeves rolled up revealing clean, tanned forearms. He didn't need a mirror to know that his hair was trimmed and face clean-shaven. His dirty, torn sneakers were new again.

The jagged underbite of a mountain range bit into the sky

from the horizon and a black speck that had to be the eagle headed toward them.

"Daddy?"

He turned.

Mindy stood in the grass, looking exactly as she did on the day Nora kicked him out, the day he'd thrown a glass of brandy across the room, calling Nora a "fucking bitchwhore."

He opened his mouth to speak but nothing came. His eyes were different, though: tears welled in them.

This dream feels so real, he thought.

"It's okay, Daddy," a little girl with dark pigtails said and approached him. Mindy. "Please don't run away this time."

Finally, he found his voice. "I had to, baby. I was in a real bad way. Had been for a long time. Mommy...." He didn't want to blame Nora and sighed. "Mommy was right to have me go."

"I'm not talking about that," Mindy said, now a woman. "I'm talking about the last time we saw each other. Two weeks ago."

"Oh." He looked away.

"Whenever I'm in Harden I look for you. I finally found you and you vanished."

"I...I didn't want to embarrass you. I think I've done that enough in your life."

Mindy smiled, tears glistening in her eyes. "You wouldn't have embarrassed me, Daddy."

That's easy for you to say, Harry thought. His heart would be in pieces when he awoke. He knew that whenever he thought of the dream he'd cry, yet it was too sweet to wake up from.

"Listen, Daddy," Mindy said. "I was walking down Newbury Street a few months back when an old woman approached me.

"She said, 'You're looking for someone.'

"I thought she was full of it, ya know? But then she began talking about *you,* Daddy. She *knew.* I don't know how but she did. Then she gave me a pencil she called 'the Morpheus pencil' and told me all I had to do was dream.

"I laughed. I mean, she sounded like that old song. But I started having strange dreams. It took me a few days to realize they were caused by the doodles and sketches I'd made with that pencil."

"Hm," Harry said. He didn't know what else to say.

"That's when I figured out what it was." Mindy's smile simultaneously lifted and broke his heart. How could *he* have helped create such a beautiful young woman? "The pencil has some kind of magic. I realized the old woman had given it to me to reunite us. That if I drew it, it would happen. So, I tried. But all I had were old photos and couldn't get the essence of the man you've become.

"I spent my next vacation in Harden. Spent a week looking for you. Everyone thought I was nuts. Hell, *I* thought I was nuts. Then I found you, but lost you again. Still, now I knew what you looked like.

"So I began drawing. It took me awhile to get to *this*," she said, raising her arms and indicated the fantastic world around them. "I wanted something that you'd recognize as our place.

"So, what do you think?"

Harry looked at Mindy a long time. Hadn't his first reaction been to remember Mindy's childhood drawings? She'd done it. The joy and hope vanished as pain throbbed through his heart. He wanted—needed—the dream to end.

"I want to wake up now," he said. "This dream hurts too much. I..."

"Daddy." Mindy grabbed his hands. Her hands were soft but strong. She got that from her mother. "This isn't just a dream."

"Of course it is," Harry said.

"I'll tell you what," Mindy said. "Tell me where you are and I'll be there by noon tomorrow."

"I'm under the Fairview Bridge," he said before he realized he would. "There's a spot, off Duncan Street, behind some bushes."

"I'll be there," she said. "Tomorrow by noon. I promise."

Mindy kissed his cheek and then faded from the dream.

Sleep's silky shroud slid off Harry and the tingling sensation of Mindy's kiss lingered on his cheek. He sat up, lower back protesting. The Fairview skyline shimmered across the river as the rising sun's orange glimmer climbed over the roofs. He sipped the flattened Pepsi.

It had only been a dream. It couldn't have been real. It would be damn foolish to think she'd really show up.

But…why would he have a dream like that? He didn't have a great imagination. But Mindy always had.

He performed his few morning rituals but didn't leave his spot under the bridge. The sun rose higher and traffic over the bridge thickened. People living their lives. He'd been among them. Once.

His heart sank as he remembered just how long he'd been apart from that world. Christ, he couldn't even dream of reuniting with his daughter in the city but in a dreamworld Mindy had created in childhood drawings. But why put him on a mountaintop? Why not just draw him in the field?

And then, an image flashed through his mind: a drawing eight-year-old Mindy had made of a man made of ovals lying on a box on top of a mountain.

That's you, Daddy, she'd said.

Why am I sleeping on top of a mountain, baby? he'd asked as his sip of whisky burned a trail down his throat and warmed his belly. He also remembered the anger throbbing through him. Anger at what? At Nora? At work? He couldn't really remember *why* he'd been angry, just the anger pulsing through his veins.

Because you're on top of the world, Daddy.

I'll always remember that, baby.

But he hadn't felt on top of the world. Never had. And he hadn't remembered his little girl's belief that he could ever be there. And now, with most of his life having passed, he realized the only person who had ever made him *feel* on top of the world had been the little girl he'd let down.

Unfocused anger. Rage at things beyond his control. Self-pity. Selfishness. These had been his undoing. The booze had been an accelerant, that was all.

As noon approached, his heartbeat quickened. It was only a dream. Things like that didn't really happen. Not at all. His little girl would not come to him. Not after all this time. Not after he'd failed so badly.

Tears ran down his face and he became acutely aware of

the bridge above him and the river to his right. He checked his watch. Five before noon.

Harry stood. It hurt too goddamn much. He didn't want it anymore.

And then movement came from the bushes, someone pushing their way through.

Harry couldn't move. He waited. And as the brush was pushed aside, a breeze like that from a mountain cooled the tears on his cheeks and he knew, at that moment, that sometimes people get a second chance.

INQUISITOR, INC.

"I want to hear her say it," Douglas Houghton said.

Hans Gerlach stared with cold, blue eyes at the doughy CEO over his glass-topped mahogany desk. Houghton fidgeted.

"The truth is my business. My life." Even after all these years, Hans had still retained his German accent. "But you have no proof?"

Houghton's pale, cream-colored face suddenly became red. Sweat beaded on his forehead and on his scalp under his wispy blondish hair.

"Isn't that what *you're* for? To make her tell me what I want to hear?"

Hans smiled. "Oh, I can make her tell you anything you want to know. I'm not concerned with that. I'm concerned with whether you understand my methods. I can be very... persuasive."

Houghton nodded, his jowls and double chin quivering. "I know what she's been doing. I can smell the fuck on her a mile away. But I don't want to hire some goddamn private detective to follow her, take pictures, and post them on the Internet. I want her to tell me herself. I want to hear her say it."

"You are quite ruthless, Mr. Houghton," Gerlach said.

Houghton tugged the lapels of his suit jacket. "You don't get to the top unless you spill a little blood."

Gerlach removed a cigarette from a gold case a president had given him and lit it, smiling. "I'm afraid you're correct on that, Mr. Houghton."

Gerlach watched Douglas Houghton get into his new BMW from his office window. He inhaled the last of his cigarette and mashed it out in a crystal ashtray. His lower back ached. He sat in the dark brown leather office chair and looked up at the ceiling. He was getting too old for this.

Although he'd been hired by politicians, entertainment people, and, on a few occasions, law enforcement agencies (both local and federal), the frosted glass of his office door didn't have his name on it. It read, simply, INQUISITOR, INC.

He sighed and looked in a manila folder marked HOUGHTON. Douglas Houghton was the CEO of an Internet firm who'd gotten rich quick in the Internet boom of the mid-nineteen-nineties and had somehow maintained his fortune through the dot-com crash of the late nineteen-nineties. Houghton hired Hans to extract information from one Mrs. Claudia Houghton, age twenty-five, blonde hair, blue eyes, and around five feet eight inches tall—taller than her husband who stood no taller than five-six. Gerlach stared at the three photos of Claudia Houghton.

The first was a wedding photo. They appeared happy. Gerlach understood that with this picture, Houghton was trying to convince him that they had once been happy. The photo was a year old but Houghton's hairline had receded significantly. The second was of Claudia in a bikini on a yacht somewhere. Gerlach believed it to be the Mediterranean; he'd visited there many times. The final photo was the most helpful. Claudia wore bluejeans and a red and black flannel shirt with a thick blue vest over it. The photo had been taken in the fall as she groomed a brown horse. She looked peaceful, serene.

The last photo gave Gerlach a chill. He didn't know why and didn't like it. However, at seventy-one, he was set in his ways and the notion of calling Houghton and canceling the arrangement never rose above his subconscious.

Unfortunately, the private detective Hans usually hired to ensure that the husband/wife didn't have some sort of vendetta against his/her spouse was on vacation out of state. He knew he should probably call in another investigator, just to be sure, form followed function after all, but it wasn't as though would-be clients could find Inquisitor, Inc. in the Yellow Pages; Gerlach's business relied solely on word-of-mouth.

The grandfather clock in the corner of the office chimed four and Gerlach closed the folder. He stood and went to an original Dalí painting that hung on the east wall. He removed the painting to reveal a number pad, punched in the code that opened a safe, and placed the Houghton file alongside a cash box filled with five hundred thousand dollars—back-up money in case something happened and he had to quickly leave town. All other files were kept in a safe hidden in the interrogation room.

Hans locked the office door behind him when he left.

The nightmare haunted Hans the way it had for sixty-one years. It was no less intense now than it had been the first night he'd had it, in Paris, under the supervision of an Allied Forces trooper who either didn't speak German or refused to.

The nightmare:

Hans was ten years old and in his father's laboratory. Screams filled the room as several Jews had acid injected into their bloodstream. Their screams were the most primal things Hans had ever heard. He felt special, though; it was the first time he'd been allowed into the laboratory to watch—and even help—his father perform der Führer's experiments.

An explosion shook the lab. Following the blast, the sound of many boots pounded down the stairs toward them. The lab door crashed inward and infantrymen streamed inside. His father put the barrel of a pistol against his left temple, looked at the Allied infantrymen, and said, "*Heil Hitler.*" Then he squeezed the trigger.

The pistol's pop echoed through time. Ten, twenty, thirty, forty, fifty, sixty years it went, from the small Polish town near the border across time and space to Boston, Massachusetts, at the beginning of the new millennium.

And it woke Hans.

It always woke Hans.

And he lay in bed, sweating and shivering. Sixty-one years. His father had lied to him. The regime had lied. No purification had taken place, for religion, color, creed meant nothing. It was truth that defined a person. And the truth was that the nightmares were almost over. He knew it. He was old.

A retirement home was on the northwest border of the Sunnybrook Stables grounds, where Claudia Houghton kept her horse. The old age home didn't interest Hans at all. That it was there proved to be a welcome coincidence, for when he appeared at the front gate of the stables' grounds, the security guard nodded, not without a little disdain, and let him enter. Hans had found his age to be a great help in his chosen profession; many people were likely to trust an old man.

He walked past other riders going to or returning from rides and smiled to a woman, who returned his smile. Several other old people walked the stable grounds, enjoying the outdoors. The smell of hay and horseshit floated through the air. Hans remained focused on his task. He was at the farthest stable when he saw her.

Claudia Houghton brushed her horse's light brown mane. It was as though he'd climbed through Houghton's photograph and a slight case of vertigo washed over Hans. Claudia Houghton wore the same clothes that she wore in the picture, her hair was tied back with the same red elastic, her head was tilted the same way.

Douglas Houghton must've been mistaken; this woman wouldn't cheat. He quickly pushed the thought out of his head. He remembered thinking the same about Marilyn Monroe way back when but the secrets she'd revealed to him were well beyond her beautiful, dim-witted façade. He hadn't been surprised when he'd awoken the next day to find she'd died not long after he'd left her to entertain other visitors, visitors armed with a little black bag and the information Hans had extracted. Number one rule to this line of work: Never let appearances fool you.

She looked up at him. His heart stopped, his feet chilled, and his flesh prickled as his mind crazily screamed, _She's onto you!_ That was impossible, of course. She couldn't know about the vial and the needle in his left coat pocket. Claudia Houghton's lips parted and she smiled. Under different circumstances, in another time, Hans believed he could have fallen in love.

"Hi," she said. "Her name is Alexis."

"That's a very pretty name," Hans said. "A beautiful specimen."

Mrs. Houghton put the brush in an empty, aluminum pail and patted the horse's dark brown rear. "Thank you. I've had her since I was fifteen. My father bought her for me."

"Your father must love you very much."

Mrs. Houghton smiled and her eyes seemed to focus on something only she could see. "You have no idea."

"Please, don't let an old fool like me stop you on this beautiful day," Hans said. "Enjoy yourself. Enjoy Alexis."

Claudia Houghton mounted her horse. "Thank you." Alexis began to move and Mrs. Houghton stopped her. "One last thing. Is your accent German?"

Hans smiled. "Yes."

"Thought so." She gave Hans one last smile. "*Tschüs.*"

Claudia Houghton rode off to the east. Once she disappeared around a bend, Hans turned and walked back toward the Sunnybrook Stables entrance where the same guard who'd allowed his entrance sat in his booth, reading *Low Rider* magazine.

"Excuse me, son," Hans said.

The guard looked up, annoyed.

"I wondered if you could flash those lights on and off twice when Claudia Houghton is leaving." He nodded to two lamps on either side of the stables' entrance.

"Why you want me to do that?" the guard asked.

On the cover of *Low Rider* Hans saw a 1963 Chevy convertible, yellow with lots of chrome. Standing near the car was a young woman in a bikini that could best be described as minimalist triangles strategically placed. He looked at the young man, arched an eyebrow, and lifted a one hundred dollar bill he'd had ready.

"No reason except to make an innocent old man happy," Hans said.

The guard stared wide-eyed at the bill. His eyes then narrowed, aware of how uncool he looked, and slowly reached and took the hundred.

"No problem, man," the guard said.

"Thank you." He began to turn around and stopped. He looked at the young man who continued to pretend to read. "One last thing, if she leaves and those lights don't go on, I'll kill your family one by one until I get to you. Understood?"

The guard looked at him, mouth agape.

Hans smiled and leaned in. "And if you tell anyone at all that I said that, I'll feed your testicles to a pack of angry Doberman Pinschers. While they're still attached to you."

Then Hans turned and left the Sunnybrook Stables. He waited in his car for two hours before the lamps near the entrance of Sunnybrook Stables flicked on and off twice. Hans smiled. He'd already called a hitman he trusted named Jake Stone to take the guard out when he got off work. There could be absolutely no connection between Hans and Sunnybrook. Hans popped the hood and got out of his car. Claudia Houghton's cranberry colored Mercedes ML320, looking like it just rolled off the showroom floor, exited through the gate.

Hans took a deep breath, exhaled, and got himself into character. He needed to look helpless, hopeless, and upset. Like one of those old men sometimes seen wandering aimlessly in parking lots, not remembering exactly where he parked. Mrs. Houghton's truck pulled out of the Sunnybrook Stables grounds and headed toward Hans. She recognized him as she approached and spent less than a moment thinking about it. Her blinker flicked on and she crossed over the yellow line, stopping her truck in front of his car.

"Is everything okay?" she asked as she got out of the truck.

"I don't know…" Hans said.

"I thought you lived at the home," she said, nodding toward the building behind some brush and up a hill.

"My sister does," Hans said. "I took my walk and was heading home when the car began acting funny. Then *I* began…" He stopped and touched his chest with his right hand. His left was in his pocket, prepping the syringe.

"Oh my god," Claudia Houghton said. "My phone's in the truck. I'll go—"

She'd turned to go back to the truck when, faster than anyone would've given him credit for, Hans removed the syringe and stuck her in the arm, depressing the plunger. In two slick moves the syringe was back in his pocket and Claudia Houghton had fallen back, into his arms. No one came up or went down the country road. He helped her into the back seat of his car and climbed into the driver's seat. He drove away from the stables with a slight smile.

The inquisition room was a soundproof room twice the size of his office. Some of its equipment were modern versions of medieval torture devices, some were things that had been created by scientists—like his father—under Hitler's employ, some had been designed for wholly different purposes—the S&M movement provided a lot of "toys" for Hans's line of work. He'd invented two things himself. Right now, none of it was used. Right now, Claudia Houghton was strapped into a dentist's chair, which worked wonders for Hans. The terror many people associated with the chair was a psychological weapon that none of the other alien-looking machines could provide. The only light in the room was a spotlight on the young woman.

Claudia Houghton looked like an apparition under the spotlight. Hans watched from a nearby stool. She'd passed out on the drive to the building and he'd had to bring her up here on his own, which had caused a sharp pain to flash through his lower back like a hot knife ripping at his delicate flesh. He should sit in the La-Z-Boy in the corner but form followed function and he was supposed to sit on the stool at this point.

Claudia Houghton's eyes fluttered open. She tried to block them from the bright light but her right arm only strained against the leather strap at her side. She soon found out that both arms, both legs, and her head were all strapped to the chair. She screamed. Long and shrill, it pierced Hans's eardrums but he didn't stop her. Mrs. Houghton was about to experience the most painful period of her life and he might as well allow her this small moment of comfort.

Her scream finally died, leaving Mrs. Houghton out of breath. Hans remained on the stool, staring. She stared back. They remained staring at each other for almost two minutes before Claudia Houghton broke the silence with clichés: *What do you want from me? Do you want my husband's money? My father is a very powerful man. You'll regret this.*

Hans said nothing.

A red light blinked over the entrance to the office, which meant someone was in the hallway.

"Please wait here," Hans said to Claudia. "I'll be right back."

Hans left her, screaming renewed. Douglas Houghton stood in the corridor outside the office, pale, wide-eyed. Sweat glistened on his forehead and a trembling hand held a bag with a change of clothes for his wife. Hans rushed Houghton inside.

"She's here?" Houghton said. "Where?"

"I called you, didn't I?" Hans said, closing and locking the office door. "Are you prepared for what's about to happen?"

"I'm ready," Houghton said. Was there excitement in his voice? No. Of course not. Nervous energy, perhaps, but not excitement.

"Very well," said Hans. "Right this way."

At this point, he revealed the inquisition room to clients. Once the clients crossed the threshold, they became an accomplice.

Claudia looked toward the open door. Hans situated the room so that the inquired would be unable to see anything more than dark shapes.

Hans said nothing as he returned to his stool. There was a moment when he thought Houghton would try to back out, which would involve a lot of nastiness, but the waxen, pudgy man finally came.

"Doug!" Claudia cried when he entered her circle of light. "Oh my god, I didn't think I'd ever see you ag—

"Wait. What are you doing here?"

Douglas Houghton stepped closer to his wife and Hans felt something in his stomach he'd never felt before. Was the feeling apprehension?

You're getting old, Hans told himself.

"I—" Houghton began.

"Uh-uh-uh," Hans said. "I'm afraid I must do all the talking, Mr. Houghton. If you'd kindly step away from your wife."

Houghton glared at Hans. After getting rich and fat off his

Internet venture, he wasn't used to being told what to do. But, even at seventy-one, Hans Gerlach was formidable. He was still tougher than Houghton would ever be. Houghton backed away.

"Now, Mrs. Houghton," Hans said. "I know you are confused. You're wondering why you're here, why your husband is here, why we're all here."

Claudia said nothing, just looked from Hans to her husband, terror filling her eyes. She realized that her husband was in on this. Again, Hans felt that pang but couldn't understand what it meant. Something told him to stop, to cancel this, but he'd gone too far to stop now.

"Your husband," Hans said, pushing himself along, "believes you are having an affair."

Claudia opened her mouth to say something but Hans raised a finger.

"You'll have your turn to speak, Mrs. Houghton," Hans said. "Now, I'm about to ask you a question. I'll give you three chances to answer it before I have to resort to my tools.

"Mrs. Houghton, are you having an affair?"

Claudia looked like he'd slapped her as painful shock filled her eyes. "No."

"Again, Mrs. Houghton." He slid on a rubber glove. "Are you having an extramarital affair?"

Her bottom lip trembled. "No."

Why? Hans wondered. *Why do they do this? They've been caught yet insist on denying it. But this time—*

Hans pushed his thoughts away. Must remain focused. "One final time, Mrs. Houghton." He put on the other glove. "Have you had sex with someone other than Mr. Houghton?"

It'd happened four times that he hadn't had to go beyond the third question. Only once had the person confessed after the first one. Why was the truth so difficult for people? Hans had spent his life wondering that.

"*No!*" she cried. "*Never!*"

Hans's hand shot out, striking her with his palm. Her hair fell into her face and she grunted.

"Have you been fucking around on your husband?"

A long sob. "*Noooo….*"

With the back of his hand. Harder this time. Hans asked again. She denied.

Hans took a pair of scissors—the kind EMTs and emergency room doctors used—and cut her shirt open. When the flannel shirt was removed, he removed the tee shirt beneath, asking between them if she were having an affair.

"Please," Claudia cried. "*Pleeeease* don't."

Topless, still strapped to the chair, she screamed three piercing screams. Hans stood back and waited. Claudia's voice cracked during the third scream and she fell silent.

Hans knelt and looked into her eyes.

"I know you are very uncomfortable," he said. "I really don't want to hurt you. But we need the truth now, Claudia. Soon I will stop asking and just go from one inspiring tool to another until you tell us the truth.

"Now, please, are you having an affair?"

A pause. Claudia shook her head, breathing heavily due to anxiety. Hans followed her pink nipples as they rose with her heaving breasts. He sighed, shook his head.

"Very well," he said and stood.

He pinched and twisted Claudia's right nipple. She screamed.

"Anytime you want to confess," Hans said. "I'll accept."

Then he twisted the left nipple. Then both. Hans undid her straps, took off the rest of her clothes, moved her to a table, and strapped her wrists and ankles to each corner. Hans glanced at Douglas Houghton occasionally but had trouble seeing the man in the gloom of the surrounding room.

"Anything you'd like to say?" Hans asked Mrs. Houghton. "No?"

For the next eight hours, Hans Gerlach inquired about Claudia Houghton's extramarital life. He used heat in different forms, he applied small volts of electricity in tender areas, he cut her, hit her, and stretched her on a rack. He used psychological tools like threatening her loved ones, though he didn't get as specific about them as he normally liked to since he hadn't been able to get his usual private investigator to look up any information on them. She wouldn't confess. Even after she'd defecated on the table after a particularly painful tool was used (one of the S&M toys, actually), through the humiliation of lying in her own stinking, steaming shit, she would not confess.

Then:

"*Ididit,*" Claudia mumbled. "*Ididitpleasestop.*"

Hans stopped, bamboo slivers in his hand, not a single one under her fingernails. His heart dropped. His feet went cold. She lied. Somehow, Hans knew *she lied.*

And then came a hitch of breath and a slight moan from the darkness, from where Douglas Houghton sat, watching.

Hans flipped a nearby light switch.

Douglas Houghton sat on the stool, caught with his penis deflating in his hand and a snail-like trail of semen dripping to the floor.

Hans looked back at Claudia. She'd been innocent. All this time she'd been innocent. Had Hans gone through proper channels, investigated her, he would've known. This never would've happened. For the first time in his career, he'd made a mistake. Form followed function and he'd fucked up.

He put the bamboo slivers back in their jar on the workbench and went to Claudia.

"I...I'm sorry," Hans said, hands trembling as he undid her straps. "Please, I...."

He looked at Douglas Houghton.

Houghton stood by the stool, arms folded, smiling. Arrogance radiated off him.

"You knew," Hans said. "You *knew* she wasn't having an affair."

"And I bet she won't now, huh?"

Hans looked at the woman, who'd curled up, trembling. She didn't cry. She was beyond tears.

"Don't tell me you don't get off on this," Houghton said. "You sick fuck. I saw things today...It was incredible."

"*Incredible?*" Hans yelled. "You call what just happened *incredible?*

"Take your wife and get out of here."

Houghton continued to smile that arrogant smile. He helped Claudia up, helped her dress in the change of clothes he'd brought with him, and helped the quivering mass of flesh that had once been Claudia Houghton away.

For the first time in sixty-one years, ever since he'd realized that his father, the party, and the world had lied to him and he'd promised himself he'd get to the truth *no matter what*, Hans Gerlach cried.

INTERNET MILLIONAIRE DEAD

The headline screamed at Hans from his desk. He'd stared at it for three hours. He'd lost count of how many times he'd read the article.

Douglas Houghton had been found dead in his offices, killed execution style, two gunshot wounds to the back of the head. His wife, daughter of suspected mafia kingpin Giovanni Ambrosi, was staying at her father's summer retreat on Martha's Vineyard. Authorities suspected a rival of Ambrosi's.

The knock on the office door came at two-thirty sharp. Hans had expected it sooner. He didn't answer it, just waited.

The door smashed open and two large men came in. A small man looking like a rat strolled in a few beats later, wanting to make an entrance.

"You know who we are?" the man asked.

Hans nodded.

"Where's the room?"

Hans indicated the door to his right.

The man took a phone from his inner coat pocket and pressed a button.

"We found him, sir…Yeah…Uh-huh…Okay." Another button and the phone disappeared. "Mr. Ambrosi will be with us shortly. He wants you to show us your playroom."

Hans stood on trembling legs and went to the door. He felt their eyes pierce him. He'd thought about blowing his brains out. He'd thought about jumping out the window. Mostly, though, he'd thought about how he wished he'd done his homework on Claudia Houghton, neé Ambrosi. He wished he'd known the truth.

Hans said nothing as he opened the door and allowed the

mobsters into his dungeon. He'd be doing a lot of talking soon, he knew, would tell them all the truths he knew. The inquisition was about to begin.

YOU MAKE MY FLESH CRAWL

Maybe love—honest, heartfelt *love*—would stop it this time, Barry told himself as he drove to Leigh's place. Meanwhile, he also cursed himself for allowing things to come this far. After Katie died, he promised himself he'd never love again. Of course, it'd taken two more deaths to convince him to keep the promise.

But you didn't really love *them,* said a rational voice, one that had been coming around a lot since he met Leigh. *Katie was your first real girlfriend. You thought you loved her at the time, but were too young to know what love was. And the other two were just one night stands. What happened to them was tragic, yes, but Leigh's different. You love her.*

But that could be the voice of self-deception. As Barry parked in front of Leigh's apartment building, he hoped not. Then his back rippled.

That's your imagination, the voice told him. *And nerves.*

"I hope so," Barry muttered and climbed out of the car.

He looked up at her apartment building. Light cast from the sunset turned the building's windows into solid gold. Leigh's apartment was on the fourth floor, the top floor, and faced this way. She could be up there watching and he wouldn't know.

Get out of here, he told himself. But he wouldn't. *Then at least control yourself.*

But...love was the thing this time. It *had* to be.

Barry entered the building and climbed the stairs to the fourth floor. Elevators made him nervous but, besides that, they were too fast. He wanted time to think. It'd been five years since he seriously considered having anything more than friendship with a woman. He'd met many women in that time, had made a few friends and had quietly suffered crushes. Throughout it all he'd been careful not to know these women too well. He'd been careful not to allow natural sexual energy to overwhelm his resolve. Somehow Leigh broke through.

Like all the women he'd befriended, she'd spoken to him first. He couldn't even remember what she'd said but he'd responded kindly, quickly noting her light blue eyes, and had left it at that. A few days later, they happened to share an elevator and talked again. This led to taking occasional lunch hours together, occasions that had steadily increased. And then, in a moment of urgent loneliness, a moment when he just didn't want to go to the movies alone again, when he needed a friend, he'd asked if she were free.

She had been.

Barry's heartbeat quickened when he reached the fourth floor. While nervous energy always coursed through his body when he and Leigh got together, this time was worse. The hall remained the same; the elevator still shared the wall with the stairwell exit and the potted palms still sat in corners. Only *he* was different, and only because he'd been so lonely for so long.

Leigh's apartment, 430, was at the end of the hall. He took a deep breath and started toward it. The corridor seemed to stretch for miles and yet he got to her apartment before he was ready.

If Leigh stood on the other side of the door, peering through the peephole, she'd probably think he'd gone insane. Barry stood with wide eyes, pale with a film of nervous perspiration on his forehead.

Knock, the rational voice told him. *Just lift your hand and knock. Simple as that.*

Go ahead, the nervous voice said. *Knock. But think before you do anything rash. Remember the others....*

Barry lifted a fist and rapped on the door. A moment later Leigh opened it, smiling. Her smile warmed him as it had since she first flashed it. Her dark red hair was held back with a clip.

"Come in," she said. "Want something to drink?"

"Water's fine," he said.

"Right for the hard stuff," she said. "Sit down. I'll be right back."

He sat on her couch. The walls had a few pieces of art along with several pictures of friends and family. He stayed at the edge of the couch, fingers twiddling. Did he sense tingling on his back? He decided not. Just nervous energy.

"Your water," Leigh said. "If you don't mind, I went with something a little stronger: ginger ale."

"Lush," he said, smiling.

"So," Leigh said as she sat beside him on the couch. "What's new?"

"Not much," he said. "You?"

"Same," she said and they laughed. "Hope you don't mind but I ordered a pizza."

"I never turn down pizza," Barry said.

Looking at him, she sipped her soda. Had her tongue just flitted against the ice cube rattling the glass? "Is everything all right?"

He blinked at the question and forced himself not to look away, though he quite badly wanted to. His brown eyes met her blue ones. "Yeah. Everything's fine. Why?"

"You're not your usual bubbly self."

That's because I'm dying here, he thought. *I want you more than I've ever wanted anyone. I want to hold you and live with you and grow old with you but...I...CAN'T!*

Why not? the rational voice asked.

"It's nothing," he said, startled by the sound of his own voice.

"Okay," Leigh said. She didn't quite believe him but let it rest.

Someone knocked on the door. "Pizza's here," she said.

She went to the small dining table, took some cash from her purse, and went to the door.

Barry brought the water to his lips with a trembling hand and sipped. The cold water felt good going down.

That's it, the rational voice said. *Cool down. Chill out.*

Leigh came back with the pizza. The aroma drifting over from the box made Barry's stomach growl.

"Chicken pizza?" he asked.

"Definitely chicken pizza," Leigh said. "Help yourself. I'll get some napkins."

Leigh went into the small kitchen and he opened the pizza box. Steam plumed out and the scent of sauce and grilled chicken wafted up to him. Barry gasped at mottled and bloody flesh that had crawled off its muscles and pulsated in the box.

He pushed himself away from the pizza and stifled a yelp. Leigh came from the kitchen with the napkins. "I'll put the movie on."

"Okay," he managed.

"Something wrong with the pizza?" she asked and lifted the top.

Grilled chicken sat on the melted cheese and sauce just as it should have. She looked from the pizza to him.

He shrugged. "I just decided to wait for you."

Again, there was suspicion in Leigh's nod, but she didn't push it. She would sooner or later, though. Leigh pointed the remote at the TV and called up the movie. Then she sat beside him and took a slice of pizza.

Barry and Leigh talked through the movie. At some point, Leigh got quite close to him, her arm touching his. A chill rolled down his spine. A chill. Not a ripple on his back. Not his flesh making some odd movement. An honest-to-god *chill*.

Soon, her head rested on his shoulder. Before he was aware that he would do it, he raised his arm and rested it on her shoulders. She snuggled closer. His flesh moved but not on his back. Barry closed his eyes and swallowed. When he opened them, he focused on the movie, not on the warmth of her hand resting on his lap.

She looked up at him and smiled. He'd seen the mischief in her eyes before, but this time there was an edge. And yet, there was something else too. A nervous energy. He noticed that one of her hands rubbed the skin on her forearm. She slowly moved closer and their lips met, lightly at first, as though she expected an explosion, then she let out a small breath and pressure mounted that numbed his lips. Her tongue flickered against his and soon they held each other.

His conscience screamed at him to stop. He didn't want it to happen again, couldn't allow it to happen again. But the need was too strong.

In a symphony of kissing, holding, caressing, groping, whispering, moaning, and gasping, they went to Leigh's bedroom, leaving a trail of clothes. She tore open a condom package and slipped it over him in a few fluid movements that didn't break their rhythm. Lying down, Leigh guided Barry and he closed his eyes as warmth surrounded him. And then he was gone, lost in the moment, the movement, the sweat, the *need*.

Even before Barry fully awoke the next morning, the first thought to enter his head was: *Nothing happened.* He felt Leigh's arm draped over him from behind. Her breath came evenly, quietly. She was an angel. She cured him. She was his savior.

He began to turn so he could face her when he noticed two things simultaneously: the exposed muscles and cartilage of his shoulder and upper arm and the exposed muscles and cartilage of Leigh's arm.

Barry screamed (without lips, his mind frantically noted) and rushed out of bed as Leigh cried out and he looked at her, expecting to see his flesh on her, tearing at her flesh as it had done with the other three in his past. What he saw instead were her blue eyes, full of fear, as she stared at him. Fear and...recognition. Barry realized she wasn't concerned for herself, but... for *him*.

A strange sound came from the floor at the foot of the bed and he looked. Leigh also looked. Their fleshes writhed together, but not devouring.

Leigh spoke first (without lips, he noted). "I never thought this would happen to me."

He looked at her, his fear disappearing as he looked into her eyes. "You...you're...."

She rose on the bed, onto her knees, and wrapped her fleshless arms around his fleshless neck.

"I knew," she said. "Somehow, I *knew*."

Heart pounding, joy pouring into Barry's heart, he kissed

her and allowed himself to be lost. Soon, they lay together again, their bodies against each other. And for the first time, they knew love; honest, heartfelt *love*.

KILL -13-

Grant Melo never thought he'd have to kill anyone, let alone one of his students. Though he didn't know it, during his fourth period class on the first day of school in his third year teaching English at Harden High, the seed was planted.

The class was an odd class in that there were only thirteen students enrolled. The usual classes ranged around twenty to thirty, usually tending toward the latter rather than the former. The kid came in and took a seat in the back of the class. His black hair was uncombed and he wore thick glasses and a black Metallica tee shirt. Scanning the thirteen students in the class, this kid stuck out. At that moment, Grant wasn't sure why and began with the tasks of introducing himself to the students and taking attendance. It was while going down the roster that he realized that the kid, whose name was Martin Collier, showed no expression. It wasn't even that this kid's face held no expression but that his eyes, behind the thick lenses he wore, were strangely vacant. Not the normal vacancy of those suffering from terminal stupidity—he'd seen plenty of that, even in only three years of teaching—but rather a deeper vacancy that Grant couldn't put his finger on.

He tried to push the uneasiness away, chalked it up to the pre-show jitters he still suffered. After he'd called attendance, not shaking the strange feeling that Martin Collier gave him, he began the first lesson.

One of the things he'd heard from students (and from teachers who heard the kids talk) was that they liked him because he was funny. It was a quality he believed also made him a good father. By the end of class, he'd had the students laughing and seemingly ready to do that night's reading (most of them wouldn't, though; he'd learned that by now). It was a huge reaction for high school seniors. Except for Martin Collier. While the kid didn't appear unpleasant, he didn't respond, either. He could've been half asleep, which was somewhat normal for teenagers in English class, but….

The fourth period students rushed out of the room. Some of them would have lunch now, others their next class. Many of them talked to each other, grumbling about the first day of school or parents or just about everything else, while Martin Collier took his books in his left hand and walked alone. He said nothing. It appeared that Martin Collier was lost in his own thoughts.

"Have a good day," Grant said, smiling.

Martin Collier's eyes shifted to him. He may have nodded, though it was hard to tell for sure, and walked out of class.

Whether his students had lunch now didn't matter much to him. What mattered was that *he* had lunch now. Even better was that today's lunch was followed by a prep period. He left the room to find a smile with light blue eyes waiting in the short corridor of the class alcove.

"How's it going?" Rita Wittner asked, standing beside her closed classroom door.

"Not bad," Grant said. "You?"

"Third period was a class full of jocks. Seniors, no less."

"Ouch. What'd you do over the summer to deserve that?"

Rita laughed. "Is it lunch for Mr. Melo?"

"It is," Grant said. "And for Ms. Wittner?"

"Sure is." Rita started teaching the year before Grant and with their classrooms in such close proximity, they'd become fast friends. Rita was a young, single blonde woman and there were sometimes whispers and teasing from some of the older, more jaded staff members about just how close their friendship had become. What none of them knew was that when Grant had begun teaching, he was going through a messy divorce. Rita, having just come out of a long relationship, had somehow sensed his troubles and had become a friend during that trying time.

On their way to the teacher's room, where a welcome-back-buffet awaited them, Grant saw Martin Collier closing his locker

and walking away. Had he glanced at Grant? if so, he'd continued on without a word or any change of facial expression.

That boy's dangerous, he thought, and then told himself he
was paranoid.

After two weeks, while things had mostly settled down, Martin
Collier still made Grant uneasy. He came to class everyday but
didn't participate. When he was called on, he often mumbled
something unintelligible. When Grant tried to get him to speak
again without mumbling, the kid would clam up. He did the
classwork but his thoughts seemed half-formed and several
assignments were turned in incomplete. The homework for the
class was mostly reading and Martin Collier's answers on the
post-reading quizzes were correct but vague. Work was often
turned in late, too, which lowered his grade. The unfinished or
late assignments were hurting the kid and Martin Collier was
failing. It would soon be time for Grant to give out progress
reports.

Right before every class for the past few days, Grant promised that *today* would be the day that he'd talk to Martin Collier.
Each day, however, Grant felt too uneasy to ask the young
man to stay behind as the rest of the class moved on. Why did
Martin Collier make him so goddamn nervous? Had he become
so square that a kid with a flat affect, who wore heavy metal tee
shirts for Metallica and Slayer and Megadeth freaked him out?

Not at all. Just Martin Collier.

The bell rang to start the school day and Grant went into
the hall to monitor. Harden High used a rotating schedule and
today's first period class was Martin Collier's. He found his
thumb and index finger rubbing together, like they had during
the bad times, and forced himself to stop, to focus on the day
ahead. Rita already stood in the hall, and smiled at Grant. Her
blue eyes were so bright they momentarily allowed Grant to forget about Martin Collier and he smiled back.

"Things okay?" she asked as the influx of students entered
the halls, bringing with it a cacophony of conversation and
clanging of lockers. "You looked a little...."

Grant shrugged. "Yeah."

"How's Ellie?"

He smiled. Thinking about his daughter made him smile, though he hadn't had her this past weekend and that made him sad. "She's fine, I guess. I'll see her this coming weekend."

Rita smiled. "You won't have her tonight?"

"No. I have a class turning in essays today so I'll be grading all night."

"Oh. That's a shame. I was going to see if you wanted to grab a bite to eat, maybe catch a movie. But if you're intent on grading papers...."

Grant looked at Rita, surprised. "I think I can push the papers back a few hours."

"Time to be Ms. Wittner and Mr. Melo." Rita smiled. "We'll solidify our plans at lunch." She went to her classroom, leaving Grant in the hall looking at the closed classroom door.

He realized the hallways were now mostly empty.

Mostly empty except for Martin Collier. He slowly walked to class, holding his books in his left hand. Grant smiled and said good morning. Martin Collier said nothing and his odd lack of expression didn't change.

He's one of those kids who'll shoot up a school.

Grant shuddered. It was paranoia, as was his general uneasiness concerning Martin Collier, it *had* to be, but the idea was so strong and so...right.

The mixture of excitement about Rita asking him out and the fear regarding Martin Collier made Grant dizzy.

Get yourself together, a rational voice told him. Grant inhaled, exhaled, and then went into his classroom.

A month later, students filled the lobby, awaiting the bell that announced the start of school. Grant wasn't sure why he was in the lobby; he usually took one of the side stairwells to his classroom in the morning. The lobby was usually too full of students, like now, and Grant had never truly been fond of large groups—

A scream. Quickly followed by another scream. And then another and then people shouted. Grant turned toward the commotion. The security people who were stationed at the welcome desk rushed forward, walkie-talkies in their hands. A rush of students swelled from the front doors and there was a loud crack that made the students' screams somehow louder. Another crack and one of the security people, a tall, skinny guy with black hair, fell back. There was another crack and a small girl with brown and blonde streaked hair and glasses lost the top of her head in a spray of blood, bone, and brain.

She fell at Grant's feet.

The crowd parted, rushing in all directions away from the front doors. Martin Collier entered with a semi-automatic rifle, an AR-15. His eyes were ebony behind his thick-lensed glasses. No whites, no irises. When he smiled, his teeth were tiny points. He raised the rifle. Staring at the small black eye of the barrel, Grant thought about Ellie as a burst of fire erupted from the eye and—

He awoke with sweat coating his body. Grant checked the alarm clock. Just past three in the morning. This was insane. His hands trembled as he wiped at his eyes. Tears. Was he crying? His heart rammed as anxiety overwhelmed his senses and he knew, with the conviction that only the silent dark that follows midnight can produce, that Martin Collier was dangerous.

Stop it, the rational voice said. *You need to stop this line of thinking. It's too much like….*

Grant didn't want to think about the past. No reason to open locked doors. He was in a different place in his life now. Happier. His bad marriage was two years over. He and his daughter had never been closer. He and Rita had been dating for a month now, and he believed they were entering (if they weren't already in) "serious" territory. He got out of bed and went to the computer in the living room. If he stayed in bed, the anxiety would just mount until it became too much to handle. Like back then.

The other feeling wouldn't go away. It insisted that Martin Collier was dangerous.

Grant met Martin Collier's father at Open House. The man looked old enough to be *Grant's* father and he suspected the boy had been adopted. It was probably a very wrong thought, but to deny it now would be lying to himself, would be crazy.

The elder Collier had curly gray hair, wore glasses, and spoke softly. There was something below this, though, something Grant sensed that made him uneasy.

"According to the progress report," Mr. Collier said. "Martin seems to be having some issues in your class."

"Yes," Grant said, grasping like hell to stay professional. His thumb frantically rubbed his index finger. What was his problem? He'd dealt with so much worse than this man. Last year, for instance, there'd been a woman who'd come barging into the room, demanding to know how *her* daughter could *possibly* have such low grades in English. "He hasn't turned in all his assignments, which have been noted. Also, he doesn't finish in-class assignments."

"Have you talked to him about this?"

"No," Grant said. "That's why I sent home the progress report...."

"I would think speaking to the boy would be easier than *this*," Mr. Collier raised the paper. "Is this school protocol? Martin's algebra teacher at least called me."

Martin Collier's algebra teacher called home? Why the hell hadn't Grant thought about asking the kid's other teachers about him? Deductive skills. He was a real fuckin' Monsieur Dupin.

"I'm sorry," Grant said. "It's not that Martin Co—" He paused a moment, then forced a cough, as though he were clearing his throat. He realized that he always thought of the boy with both names—Martin Collier—not Martin, not Marty, not even Collier. Martin Collier. "Excuse me. It's not that Martin's disruptive in any way. I was hoping the progress report would provide a sort of spark. If a change hadn't come up soon, I would've called you."

Grant couldn't remember the last time he'd lied like that. Why would he even have to? The kid was a goddamn senior in high school! Less than a year away from graduation.

"I see," the elder Collier said.

Does he really, though? Does he see that his son is dangerous and will probably take him out before he comes to school to take out the rest of us?

"Well, please *do* let me know how Marty's academics progress from here," Mr. Collier said. "I'll do everything in my power to make sure Marty stays on the proper path."

The proper path. The Proper Path. Just what, in Old Man Collier's mind, was the Proper Path? Was it the same path that many of the other parents who'd come to see him wanted their children to walk along? A simple metaphor that meant achieving good grades with the hope of attending a good college and possibly a good career or medical/law school? How did Mr. Collier keep his son on the Proper Path? Rewards? Threats? Beatings? No, Mr. Collier wouldn't lay a hand on his son, he'd speak to him. His quiet voice would cut through every other sound sharper and cleaner than any shout could ever hope to do. It had probably started when Martin Collier was no more than a toddler.

"No, Martin. One does not point at the fat lady."

Or:

"No, Martin. One does not scream when one does not get one's way."

Gently pushing, gently leaning on Martin Collier until the boy, by the fourth grade, had introverted, had rebelled because by now the other kids were beginning to sense that something was different about him, something was *wrong* about him. Sometime before he'd begun high school (but not too long before), Martin Collier began to quietly rebel against his father. Grades slipping. Heavy metal music. Heavy metal, unlike the other popular rebellious music—rap—was like a wall of sound that Martin Collier was able to build around himself. As high school progressed and his peers saw him as an outsider, he lost more and more of his connection to the world around him. And now he was in his senior year. Now he had less than a month to decide what he wanted to go to college for or if he even *wanted* to go to college, what he wanted to spend the rest of his life doing. How could he stay on the Proper Path when that path seemed to go in directions he didn't want to travel? There was only one thing to do. He'd show them. He'd show them all. Fuck their paths. Fuck their shared, stupid dreams. Fuck *them*! He'd show them, all right.

After Open House, Martin Collier's work ethic improved a little. The assignments that Martin Collier turned in were complete, his quizzes had a little more detail in their answers, but he still remained silent in class, not speaking when he was called on, barely making eye contact. He entered the room alone. He sat in the back of the room, staring off when he was supposed to be reading or writing. He left class alone. Grant had seen Martin Collier alone in the halls, no friends, that vacant, somehow insidious, look on his face.

Grant found out Martin Collier's algebra teacher was Stephanie Joyce. She'd begun teaching at Harden High the year before he had. She had shortish black hair and wore trendy sixties-style horn-rimmed glasses. He and she weren't friends so much as friendly acquaintances, able to smile at each other in the halls and hold short conversations.

"Martin Collier?" she asked when Grant saw her in the teachers' room. "He's a quiet kid. Keeps to himself. Was a little sluggish about his work but I called his father and things have been better in that regard."

"Do you sense anything...*weird* about him?"

Stephanie thought a moment. "Like I said, he's very quiet, but he's in a class with several clowns so I have my hands full...."

Grant knew that would be all from her. She didn't sense anything beyond the normal. And why should she? This was *his* paranoid delusion, wasn't it?

The rush of students pushed at him as the firecrackers went off in the cafeteria. Grant knew he should turn and run with the throng—he didn't want Ellie growing up without a father—but he couldn't. He *needed* to see it with his own eyes. And soon he was rewarded. Martin Collier, armed with an AR-15, made his way through the chaos, shooting at random students, faculty, and staff.

Grant!

He looked over and saw Rita push through students toward

him. A crack from the rifle and the top of her head sprayed off; gone was her blonde hair that he loved to run his fingers through. Her blue eyes widened in surprised fear, and then rolled up as she fell to the floor, lifeless.

And everything stopped.

Children were frozen with looks of terror on their faces. Other teachers also froze, also frightened for their lives. A teaching assistant lay on the floor, a puddle of blood below him, frozen from spreading. A tray with cereal hung in mid-air from its fall off a table, the milk splashing up with bits of Cheerios in it, unmoving. Several students who were being pushed down by the flow of panicked classmates hung in mid-air. Everything frozen.

Except Grant and Martin Collier, who stared at him.

Grant's heart rammed and he wanted to turn away from Martin Collier. Blood had spattered the boy's face and made his glasses red, like cheap sunglasses. Martin Collier walked slowly through the frozen people. A grin widened on his face, revealing tiny sharp teeth. He opened his mouth and a long, forked tongue came out and wiggled at Grant, who only then became aware that the boy wore a Kiss tee shirt. Gene Simmons had his tongue out, and so did Martin Collier. The flesh on the boy's face rippled and horns pushed their way through his mussed hair. Grant heard the grinding of bones and the wet tearing of flesh as the horns grew.

(wake up)

You can't stop me, Martin Collier said, his voice devoid of any emotion.

(wake the fuck up now)

You can try, but you can't. His voice crackled as he spoke, becoming deeper,

(wakeupwakeupwakeupwake)

until finally: *You'll NEVER BE ABLE TO SUCCEED.*

(WAKE UP!!!)

Martin Collier raised the rifle, the muzzle in Grant's face, and squeezed the trigger.

It popped and Rita and Ellie screamed, then laughed.

"Oops," said the Balloon Man at the Children's Museum. "I hate it when I do that."

"Happen often?" Rita asked.

"Too much for my liking," the Balloon Man said with a smile.

Grant watched Ellie and Rita. This was their first meeting and things were going great. The smiles and laughter were almost immediate as they drove to the Children's Museum. It was good, as good as anything that had happened to Grant in the last few years. He watched the Balloon Man make Ellie a balloon monkey, Grant's thumb and pointing finger frantically rubbing together. He found himself sneaking glances around him, even jumping at unexpected noises. The balloon popping had almost made him shout. Flashes of the nightmare he'd had the night before came to him.

Grant couldn't remember anything specific about the nightmare, but remembered enough to make him even more uneasy about Martin Collier. He tried his damnedest to convince himself that it was simple paranoia, just like around the time his marriage broke up. He didn't like to remember those days and pushed them from his mind. Maybe he'd allow those thoughts to come later this weekend, once Ellie had gone back to Alicia, once Rita was back at her place, once Grant was alone.

"Look, Daddy!" Ellie held up the balloon monkey. "It's you."

"Keep it up," Grant said. "And I'm gonna kick your butt."

Ellie giggled and Grant looked at Rita. She smiled at him and his heart pitter-pattered. The Rita Heartbeat, he called it. He was definitely in love. And judging by the way Rita took his hand and squeezed it, still looking in his eyes, so was she.

Grant was introducing the discussion of paranoia in Edgar Allan Poe's "The Tell-Tale Heart" (an irony that Grant wholly noted as he'd made up the lesson plan) when Martin Collier pointed a finger with his thumb up at the student seated in front of him, and then brought the thumb down, pretending his hand was a gun. Whatever Grant meant to say was forgotten and he stood in front of the class, his mouth instantly dry, and cold sweat broke out over his forehead.

"Mr. Melo?" Melissa Landon said from the front row. "Are you all right?"

Grant blinked away the sense of vertigo, the sense that not only was everyone in the room looking at him (of course they were, he was their teacher), but that they were soon-to-be victims. When he looked at Melissa, a beautiful young woman, with long brown hair, dark brown eyes, wearing a light blue sweater, and who always had a smile on her face (except for right now, she looked frightened because her teacher was suddenly acting *very* weird), he could see her sprawled on the desk, her head broken open to reveal what remained of her very good brain, her usually vibrant eyes staring vacantly at the ceiling tiles, blood messing her light blue sweater. Her friend, Kara Santos, sat nearby with a hole in her chest. As Grant swept the room with his eyes, he saw the rest of his students sprawled about with various parts of them blown away. All of them slaughtered. All of them except for Martin Collier.

The image of the slaughter happened in an instant.

In that instant, all was silent, except for his heartbeat, which echoed in his ears like a drum in a tomb. He forced a smile. "I'm fine," he answered Melissa, aware of his thumb rubbing his finger and made it stop. "Sorry. Mind wandered for a moment."

A kid in the back of the room, on the side opposite from where Martin Collier sat, made a wiseass comment, which produced a few chuckles, and Grant raised his copy of the textbook.

"Anyway," he said, trying to recompose himself. "'The Tell-Tale Heart' begins:

"'*TRUE!—nervous—very, very dreadfully nervous I had been and am; but why will you say that I am mad?*'"

He gulped, and smiled at the class.

"As you can see," he said. "Poe already sets up the story *in the very first line.*"

The class seemed to have enjoyed the story and as the discussion progressed, they forgot about the small digression. From that point on, though, Grant hid his fear quite well.

As December crept toward Christmas, as plans were made about families meeting new significant others, the sense of impending doom increased. On the Tuesday night in the second week of the month, tears overcame Grant after Alicia had picked up Ellie. He sobbed, unable to stop, as his apartment walls seemed too large without Ellie, but too small for him. Leaving his apartment to go somewhere more open was an option, but that could be too dangerous. Martin Collier might be out there and seeing Grant in a place other than school could set the boy off.

Grant *knew* he was the only one who sensed anything wrong with the boy. The guidance department had no history on him. His grades had always been a little below average and now he showed no signs of going to college and may not care about his grades. No teachers had reported any behavioral discrepancies. There was no hint of any mental instability in Martin Collier's past. When the guidance counselor asked Grant if anything had happened in class or through the boy's writing to provoke such questions, Grant said that nothing outright had happened, and hoped he didn't sound crazy. And as each day passed, Grant grew more certain in his belief that Martin Collier was planning something bad. He now believed Martin Collier *purposefully* didn't look at him. And on the rare occasion when Martin Collier's vacant blue eyes looked through the thick glasses at him, Grant almost *felt* the AR-15's slug smash through his chest. Still, there was no evidence to back up any of the bad feelings or paranoia he felt.

This is all you, a rational voice told him. *The boy is harmless.*

It was December, though, and the boy *still* didn't appear to have any friends. He *still* didn't speak to anyone in class, and when Grant saw the boy in the corridor during passing periods, he *still* walked alone.

Grant watched Alicia drive off with Ellie, locked his apartment door, and fell into a whirlpool of tears. He found himself on the floor, rubbing his wet eyes, snot and spit mixing with his tears. This hadn't happened since the separation, when he'd finally had to go Talk To Someone. Things were supposed to be better now, though. He had a better job, a promising new relationship—things looked great for him and his daughter. Only now, instead of the guilt of a failed marriage on his shoulders, the knowledge that Martin Collier would be the next one to appear on the news after shooting up his school was the burden that Grant couldn't handle.

But you don't know, he told himself. *You just don't* know.

He was wrong. Martin Collier was *not* the next student to be on the news for shooting up his school. That honor went, instead, to Michael Cramer in Hobneck, Maine, a small town not far from Derry. Two students were killed, three more and a teacher were wounded. Cramer then shot himself. It made national news not only because it was such a small town in Maine, but because there was nothing else going on in the world. It was in the news for only a few days since it wasn't tragic enough for the talking heads at the twenty-four-hour news channels.

That was fine, though. The details didn't matter. What mattered to Grant were the similarities between the case and Grant's life. Grant read and studied every item that appeared on the various news sites. Cramer had a Tumblr page that Grant went to (before it was shut down) and was blasted with music from Pantera. The logos for Metallica, Slayer, Megadeth, and other heavy and death metal bands adorned the page. Not that this mattered, Grant knew. He loved Metallica himself, though he wasn't fond of the other bands. Still, it did seem to be a thing between Michael Cramer and Martin Collier. His last blog entry was called "Watch Me On the News Tonight, Motherfuckers" and read simply:

Bang!

Michael Cramer was dirty blond and blue-eyed. Grant recognized the look in those eyes as the same vacant look in Martin Collier's. They shared the same initials. They even lived in similarly named places; Martin Collier in Harden, Massachusetts, and Michael Cramer in Hobneck, Maine.

Rita could tell that the news of the shooting in Maine upset Grant. She hugged him and told him it would be okay. Then, after a moment's hesitation, "Is anything else wrong?"

Grant looked at her, stopping his thumb and forefinger tango. "No. Why?"

"You haven't been yourself lately."

Grant had no reply. He put on his best sheepish smile and

shrugged, hoping it looked carefree, hoping it looked natural. Hoping Rita didn't notice how his fidgeting had grown a little more after the question. Judging by Rita's expression, the sheepish smile didn't look natural and she probably noted his fidgeting, too.

"Daddy? Can we go to the park?"

"Another day, hon."

"What'cha doin'?"

"Working."

"School stuff?"

"Yeah."

"Why are those people crying?"

Grant looked away from the photographs of the Maine shooting and looked at Ellie. She stood with her arms at her side, the reflection of his computer screen on her glasses. He forced a smile, trying to reassure her.

"Someone did something bad to them," he said. "That's all."

"So why are you looking at it for school?"

"Because," Grant said. "I don't want it to happen again."

Michael Cramer.

Martin Collier.

Hobneck, Maine.

Harden, Massachusetts.

Christmas vacation came. Almost two weeks without having to face Martin Collier. And yet, Grant couldn't stop thinking about him. Rita had begun asking him how he felt a lot, and he told her fine, but she was behaving a bit differently now. More distant. Could he blame her? He was a fucking madman.

Still, Rita went to Grant's family's house on Christmas Eve. He had Ellie that night until ten. His sister, Lori, and her family were there. His nieces and nephew ran around with Ellie, all of them laughing and excited about their new toys. Lori and Rita got along great and things felt right. His father talked to his brother-in-law, Dawson, about fishing while his mother sat drinking eggnog and enjoying her family's company.

Throughout the night, Grant's mind wandered to Martin

Collier. This wouldn't be a good Christmas for him. His father would still be upset that his boy wasn't on the Proper Path and would use the boy's Christmas as a means for punishment. This would set Martin Collier over the edge, and at some point over vacation, he'd sneak into his father's bedroom, open the closet, and find the rifle—

He stopped. Grant's father had a gun. Or at least he used to.

Before he knew he would, Grant left the doorway in which he'd been standing and quietly made his way upstairs.

His father's den had once been Lori's bedroom. Grant had helped his father fix the place up the summer Lori got married. It was then that he'd come across the gun and it became one of the many topics that they didn't see eye-to-eye. Grant believed guns were stupid in civilized society and that the ease with which they could be gotten was reflected in. the crime rate. Now, as he opened his father's desk drawer and saw the nickel-plated revolver, Grant knew he'd been correct. If guns weren't so easily accessible, Martin Collier wouldn't have access to one and neither would Grant. Lucky for Grant, his father thought otherwise. Lucky for Harden High, and for the parents of who knew how many students, Grant would be able to stop anything truly terrible from happening.

The gun went into his pants and he quietly went back downstairs and to the car, hiding the gun in his trunk with the spare tire, under carpeting. He returned to the festivities without his absence being noticed.

Later that night, after Ellie had gone home, when Grant and Rita went back to his apartment, he brought the gun inside and hid it, all under Rita's nose. She'd drunk a little too much wine at his parents' and was a little tipsy. Not bad, but enough to be *very* happy. They made love and went to sleep.

Instead of sugar-plums, Grant saw Martin Collier in a basement room, walls painted black, posters of metal bands from the late-seventies through the late-eighties adorning the walls around the dark room. The boy wiping down the AR-15. He had a faint smile on his normally dull face. After all, happiness was a warm gun.

But then Grant was no longer in the basement room but in

the school lobby with students and teachers walking through it wearing coats. Wet, slushy footprints covered the polished brick floor near the main doors. A scream erupted across from Grant, followed by a pop. He saw the flash of fire that accompanied it and then there was a rush of students pushing toward the main entrance. Above the screaming, which quickly dulled as time froze, there came a deep laughter. Then the only person who moved normally amongst the frozen people was Martin Collier.

He walked in Grant's direction, stopping to shoot random frozen classmates and faculty as he went.

You think you can stop me? the kid yelled in a voice not his own. Grant saw the horns and glowing red eyes that were the true Martin Collier. *Do you* really *think you can stop me?*

He pointed the rifle at Grant.

January third, fucker.

And he fired.

January 3rd was the second day after Christmas vacation. After that last nightmare, Grant had found himself calm on the surface. He knew now, beyond a shadow of a doubt, what he needed to do. Especially when the final piece fell before him while he was correcting papers.

They'd begun studying poetry before the vacation and his classes had been assigned to write poems. The poems had been turned in before vacation and Grant had had every intention of correcting them earlier than two days before they went back, yet here he was on New Year's Eve, correcting the poems. Rita would be coming over soon and they were supposed to spend a quiet night inside.

But before Rita showed up, he had his students' poems. There were a few good poems from the usual suspects, two great poems from unlikely sources, and the normal amount of blah or horrible poetry from mostly everyone else. And then there was Martin Collier's poem.

Knights run, bloody, into battle
Inside, a princess waits
Longing for the one she wants
Loving from afar.
-13-

It surprised Grant. It was better than most of the work that Martin Collier had done all year. Maybe he'd been wrong. Maybe Martin Collier was just an *extremely* quiet kid who didn't care enough about school to try too hard. Still, Grant's eye kept falling on the word *bloody*. And the odd 13 Martin Collier had tacked to the end of his poem. What was *that* about? He put the poem aside and tried to go onto others, but his eyes kept returning to Martin Collier's poem. And then, by accident, he saw it.

His mouth went dry and he dropped his pen. His feet went cold. His heart rammed. It was right there in his goddamn poem. A fucking confession. The first letter of each line spelled it all out: *KILL*.

This is fucking ridiculous, he told himself. *It can't be.*

But there it was. And the *13*? 13. 1/3. January 3rd. The fucking date. Or (maybe more accurately) the students in the class. Thirteen students. Or twelve students and a teacher. Right... *there.*

School resumed on January 2nd. Martin Collier was not in school. No one knew about the gun in Grant's briefcase. Not Rita, not anyone. She and he had had a great few days before returning to school. Now that Grant had a plan, he no longer worried. He knew exactly what he must do, and why. He wasn't happy about it, though. He abhorred violence but knew he was the only one who saw what Martin Collier was capable of. He was the only one.

January 3rd came. Grant didn't sleep the night before. He watched the sun rise from his kitchen window, sipping coffee. He took a shower, the hot water cleansing him. He didn't know if he'd live beyond this day. Hell, he could be dead by mid-morning. Or earlier. He sat at his desk, took the Waterman fountain pen that Rita had given him for Christmas, and wrote a letter to Ellie. And then he wrote another to Rita. He addressed each envelope and left them on his desk. He'd told Rita he needed the night to correct papers and to run something over to his ex's house, so she hadn't stayed over. He wished now that they'd made love one final time.

Dressed in his normal work clothes, he checked the gun. Fully loaded. His hand trembled as his thumb rubbed his index finger. How many lives would be lost if he didn't perform this one act of courage? All his life he'd been afraid. His fear had led him into his marriage to Alicia. His fear had caused him to have a mild nervous breakdown during the separation and divorce. His fear had held him back from dating Rita sooner than when she'd finally asked. The time for fear was over. Now was the time for action.

KILL -13-.

"Not on my watch," Grant said.

He placed the gun in his briefcase, snapped it closed, and left his apartment.

ICARUS FALLING

TO: SPACE CRUISER PM-10
FROM: SPACE STATION ICARUS
25 OCTOBER 2045
20:44:39

I'm not exactly sure how it started. At this point, it's irrelevant. At least to me. I do, however, know what happened and will happen. It seems the very name of this small, skeletal space station foretold our fate. In a sense, we got too damn close to the sun, our wings melted, and now we're falling.

Two days ago, with permission granted from Earthbase, we captured a portion of meteor. The coordinates have been recorded and transmitted elsewhere. I'll just say we captured the portion of meteor in a force field created by the KAR-678 and CE-4498 satellites.

The five of us should have been more careful once we had the meteor, which looked like a dried, shrunken tumor. We should have treated it more like the alien artifact it was. Even Dr. Henner, in all her scientific wisdom and by-the-book attitude, wasn't cautious enough with the bloody thing.

Joseph Reed and myself brought the blackened meteor to Dr. Henner's tomb-like laboratory and placed it in the observation vacuum for tests. We took our grimy gloves off and dropped them into the cleaner. Joseph rushed to the computer room, what we call Grand Central, and eagerly awaited a transmission from his wife and son. My heart went with him and envy(?) momentarily struck me. I had lost my own family when their shuttle to Moonbase crashed. I went and joined Kathryn Seagle and Norman Mitchell for lunch. The rest of the day went without incident.

Yesterday was when the incidents started. Dr. Henner was very irritable at breakfast, snapping at each of us at least once. She snapped at Norman a few times; his constant joking was getting on her nerves. Then, about an hour after our anti-gravity exercises, Norman and I were finishing up some paperwork when we heard Dr. Henner yelling. We looked at each other and then followed the yelling to the kitchen area.

"I'm *sorry*," Kathryn was saying, close to tears but too surprised to actually cry.

"It's too late to be sorry," Henner shouted. "It was the last peach yogurt and you ate it."

I saw a smile spread on Norman's face.

"We can put a request in with Supplies for—" Kathryn began.

"The next shipment of supplies isn't for *three weeks*," Henner said in a harsh, cold voice. "I wanted the yogurt *now*."

"Calm down," Norman said and placed a dark brown hand on Henner's powder blue shoulder. He was ready to laugh. "It's only yogurt."

Henner turned around and stabbed him with her icy blue eyes. Whether he noticed the rough patch of skin on the right corner of her mouth, I'll never know, but the smile that had been on Norman's face vanished.

Then Henner whipped her attention on me and I went cold. I was shocked by the rage that engulfed her. There were no signs of the woman who cried during Disney films.

Dr. Henner shot final, hateful glances at each of us and went back to her cubicle.

Norman and I looked at each other.

"What just happened?" he asked me.

"I wish I knew," I said.

"Over *yogurt*," he said, shaking his head and smiling. "I'm going to talk to the good doctor."

"Be careful," I said. "She looked…"

"Dangerous," he finished, smile gone. "Yeah, I know."

I decided to check on Kathryn. She was in her cubicle, floating over her cot and hugging her pillow.

"Five months in space doing minor experiments can be tough on some people," I said, approaching her. "It's okay. She just had a moment. She'll apologize later."

If there is a later, my mind said and I pushed the thought away.

Kathryn looked at me as if she had heard the thought. A hint of fear was in her eyes.

"If it had been something just pent-up, that would be fine," Kathryn said. "I can handle that. But she was really pissed off. If you and Norman hadn't shown up she probably would have hurt me."

I wanted to tell her she was imagining that, but couldn't. Truth was that despite how out-of-character this whole thing was for Dr. Henner, she *had* looked that upset.

"And did you notice that…sore?" Kathryn asked. "Right next to her mouth? It was bubbly, ripply."

I nodded.

There was a moment of silence. I didn't know what to say. I had come to try to comfort Kathryn but found I was unable to do so.

"I'll be all right," Kathryn said, sensing my unease.

Not long after that, I was at the observation window staring at the golf ball sized Earth and even smaller moon. The planet and its satellite glowed bright and looked warm compared to the dark, cool space station. I was sighing out already-recycled air when Norman found me.

"I think the good doctor is sick," he said.

"Why's tha—?" was all I got to when I turned and saw the bruised bump on his cheekbone. "What the hell happened?"

"She hit me," Norman said. "Hard."

That's when Joseph found us.

"I saw Kathryn at Grand Central writing a letter to Nana. She looked like she'd been crying so I asked if something was wrong," he was saying. "She said to come ask you t—Holy Christ, what happened to you?" He'd seen Norman's battle mark.

We told Joseph the story. Then we found Kathryn and dis-cussed what we should so. I said I would write and transmit the reports. After we all agreed that Dr. Henner had probably received some bad news in her most recent e-mail and was just coping with it badly, we went to bed. I think now we were all in denial.

At 03:15, screaming woke me. I unstrapped myself from my cot and went into the dark corridor. Disheveled and startled, Kathryn and Joseph soon appeared from their cubicles. We looked at each other.

"Norman," Joseph said tightly and we launched ourselves down the corridor to Norman's cubicle.

Dr. Henner, or whatever she had become, was in the cubicle. We knew it had been her because some of her curly black hair remained and the creature was wearing her powder blue coveralls. The monster's flesh was mangled and bubbled, pus oozed from some spots. The eyes were red, hands turned into talons. They gouged Norman's eyes, went into his screaming mouth, and yanked his face off.

Gore floated throughout the cubicle. Joseph lost his supper in a ball of vomit. Kathryn gasped. I somehow picked all this up as I fought my own body to control my functions. The creature that had been Dr. Elizabeth Henner, winner of humanitarian as well as science prizes, turned and looked at us with deadly red eyes.

It swiped a talon at us. I felt a swish of air as it came within millimeters of my face. Kathryn left the cubicle and I followed closely.

Joseph yelled out in pain. I turned and he rushed out of the cubicle, his right shoulder shredded. The hairs on my neck rose and my scrotum tightened as I saw the bloodied talon rise above Joseph, ready to make the kill. I grabbed him by his tee shirt and pushed off the corridor's gray rounded wall with my feet. We dashed down the corridor, away from the monster.

I looked around for Kathryn but didn't see her. The Henner-monster came out of Norman's cubicle and groaned. Pulling Joseph along behind me, my heart racing, we went through the corridor. The utility room would have tools to protect us so I headed there.

Kathryn was leaving the utility room and pushed us aside

as we entered. Apparently, she felt the same way I did about the room and its possible weapons. I pushed Joseph into the room and turned around.

The Henner-thing howled as it flew down the corridor toward Kathryn. It was five feet away from Kathryn when there was a blinding blue flash. The Henner-creature's head disintegrated. Kathryn had grabbed the TG677 laser welder/rock splitter.

I stayed where I was, trembling, not knowing what to do. Henner's (or the creature's, I guess) body floated there, headless. Kathryn turned to me a few moments later. Her eyes were red and puffy but she had stopped crying. I thought for a moment that tears would overcome me as well but they didn't. After my family's death, crying for anything else was just too damned hard.

"Let's go check on Joseph," she said.

I nodded, still unable to speak with any intelligence, and we went to the utility room.

Joseph hung there, face pale, staring at his shoulder. His bottom lip quivered. He looked up at us quickly, then back at his shoulder.

"Marie," he moaned. "I don't know if she'll understand. She'll see the scar. I told her we'd be safe on the space station. I *promised*. And Little Joe, what will I tell him? He'll have nightmares for years."

Kathryn took hold of Joseph and looked at me.

"Take Henner's body," she said. "Put it in the freezer. Then go to Grand Central and send a transmission to both the Earth and moon bases."

I nodded and went back into the corridor. Gore splattered the walls, floor, and ceiling. Recycled air pushed the metallic smell of bloody meat, mixed with human waste, through the corridor. Trying my hardest not to let it bother me, I started toward the freezer with the doctor's body. Behind me, Kathryn and Joseph went down to the med-center.

I locked Henner's body in the freezer and rushed to the lavatory just in time to vomit. That done, I went to Grand Central. I stared at the flashing cursor for a long time. Whether I knew it would be no use or just assumed (or, deep inside, even hoped), I don't know. But instead of transmitting a report, I shut the computer off.

At the med-center, Kathryn had strapped Joseph into a cot and had begun the fixings.

"Did you send the message?" she asked.

"Yes," I lied.

"I don't feel well," Joseph moaned.

"That's because you're hurt," Kathryn said. "Like Nana used to say when I hurt myself, 'We'll have you fixed up as good as new in a jiffy, kiddo.'"

"No," Joseph said and strained his neck to look at the both of us. "I woke up before...you know. My stomach hurts and I'm itchy all over."

He brought his knee up and scratched it. That's when I saw the bubbled, mangled flesh on him. He was scratching at it. Kathryn saw the grotesque flesh as well because she looked from the itchy knee to me. Her eyes said everything.

We tried to calm Joseph down and then locked him in the med-center. We went to the kitchen and Kathryn fixed us both tea. I let it out of the tube a drop at a time, watching it wobbly float around as I imagined a virus germ might before I caught and swallowed it.

"Joseph's got it," Kathryn said softly. "Whatever Dr. Henner had he's got."

"We're probably going to get it, too," I said. "If we don't already have it."

She looked at me with tired, fearful eyes. I thought she might cry.

"What do you think it is?" she asked.

I thought about it for a short time as goosebumps ran over my flesh.

"A virus of some sort," I said, watching another drop of tea wobble toward me. "And I think it came from the meteor."

She looked at me. "Is that possible?"

"Anything's possible," I said. "If a moon shuttle can crash—"

"Please don't drag them into this," Kathryn said and placed her hand on one of mine. "It was an accident. Not proof of everything that's wrong with the universe. Let them rest."

I bit into my inner cheeks to quench the anger. With the taste of blood on my tongue, I looked into my lap.

Kathryn knew that the meteor was the only foreign object in our small environment. She also knew that Dr. Henner really got into her work and had probably exposed herself to something on the meteor.

"What if we get it?" she asked me.

"We should lock ourselves into our cubicles, now, and wait. Twenty-four hours, at least. If we don't start mutating by then, we'll call for help. If one mutates before the other, though, and you see yourself starting to change, then we destroy the space station. Okay?"

"But we should call for help and—"

"And what? What if it *is* from the meteor? Earth's not going to have anything that can help us. Whoever comes here will get contaminated and bring it back with them. It could kill the human race."

Kathryn stared at me. At that moment, she hated me. Knowing I was right made her hate me even more.

We started to our cubicles when Joseph began pounding on the med-center door, swearing, threatening, begging to be let out. Kathryn and I ignored it as best we could. Neither looked at the other. Joseph was mutating and there was nothing we could do.

Quietly sobbing, Kathryn locked herself in her cubicle first. I took a shaky breath and went to the utility room. I grabbed the TG677 and went to my cubicle. It had done a great job of protecting Kathryn earlier and it made me feel a little safer. If I was going to die then I was going to do it on my own terms and not from some monster that had once been a friend.

Joseph continued yelling, screaming, and banging against the door. As time passed, the yells and screams became grunts and howls. A few times I almost went to the med-center, opened the door, and blew him out of this dark universe.

It was almost midnight, early this morning. Joseph and my stomach were howling together when new howls joined in. Kathryn had quietly mutated. Her quiet time was over. I thought of her Nana, who I never met but feel like I know because of all the times Kathryn spoke of her. They'd been planning on getting together in January, after we returned home. There would be no January now.

I made the decision at that moment to go and put them out of their misery. I felt fine except for fear and that nagging pull in my stomach that insisted on telling me I was past the point for hoping. There were none of those mish-mashes of flesh on me. No stomach ache, no itching.

I turned on the laser and was about to open my cubicle door when I heard a crash from the corridor. I leaped back, gasping.

A creature roared. It was followed by another crash, another roar. Then they began fighting. They banged around the corridor, grunting, howling, shrieking. Every now and then a human word came from one or the other. That was the worst. My skin crawled and goosebumps broke anew each time a word escaped the creatures' mouths. Their voices had lost all human tones.

The fighting continued almost an hour when one of them let out a loud, whistling shriek. The other fell silent. I had pushed myself as far back against the wall to the left of the door as was possible. Quivering, I listened. Nothing from the corridor. One had killed the other and was ready for me.

Then the victor crashed against my door.

I lost it and started screaming. I screamed for my dead wife and daughter, my parents, God, Allah, Buddha, and anyone else I thought might help me. I begged the thing to just leave me the fuck alone if it had *any* shred of humanity left in it.

It did not. It howled on the other side of the door and the crashing increased.

I calmed myself the best I could under the circumstances and started thinking. I needed a way out. I realized that in my depression brought on by losing my wife and daughter I had been secretly hoping for something like this to happen. Some tragedy. Of course, this psychological puzzle couldn't have been solved sooner to regain my love of life. Before I had passed the turning point. A plan formed, nonetheless. Not a great one but one I thought could work.

I checked the TG677 and it was still on and full of power. I closed my eyes, took a deep breath, and opened the door.

The door crashed open in front of me and hid me for a moment. The mutated Kathryn had been the victor and was now in my cubicle, tearing my cot apart.

I aimed the laser at it. Its taloned arm shot out, knocking the makeshift weapon out of my hands. The force was enough to throw me into the death-smelling corridor. The door closed and the beast crashed into it. I went toward the utility room as the monster erupted out of my cubicle, howling. I swear I heard my name in the howl.

In the utility room, I grabbed a small laser welder/cutter. This one was usually used for minor repairs inside *Icarus*. I was beginning to look for something with more power when the monster lunged into the room. I would need to get in close to do any real damage with the small laser so I grabbed a plasteel shield.

A talon broke through the plasteel shield as if it were made from paper instead of a plastic-steel combination.

I raised the laser and pressed the button. A red beam shot out and hit the monster in the center of its forehead, melting away flesh. It howled in pain and tried to grab me. The beam burned a path from its forehead, down the cheek, and to its neck. The stink of burnt flesh filled the already rancid air. Blood poured as the neck opened. The Kathryn-beast grabbed its throat, gurgling. It got away from me, one talon still stuck in the shield, and curled into a corner where it died moments later.

Shaking all over, almost completely numb, I went to the observation windows. I saw the blood red dot that was Mars to my right and the blue dot of Earth to my left. I settled on Earth until I saw your spacecraft coming toward *Icarus*.

I had been itchy for a while by then.

I came to Grand Central and saw that before she became sick, Kathryn sent an S.O.S. to Earth. I went back to my cubicle, took the TG677, and came back here. Then I started this, the final report from *Icarus*. I'm sitting here, staring at the last photograph I took with my family. My colleagues' blood and innards are floating around me. I'm caring less and less. Do you have any idea how hard it is to type as your fingers are coming together to form a talon? Of course you don't.

After I end this transmission, I will take the TG677 and puncture a wall to the outside. This way, I am sure no one else will suffer like we did. Like I am. God, the itching.

>>>END TRANSMISSION<<<

BURNED OUT

The smell of the charred remains of their house, their dream, the single object for which they'd worked so hard, lingered in Elliot Marshall's mind long beyond the time in which it should've faded. In less than two hours on that night three years earlier, the culmination of ten years hard work and dreaming was gone. His life was gone. Everything lost because…just because.

It had been just past ten that night. Kathy lay in her crib, asleep. Faye sat in the living room watching *ER* while Elliot sat in his study in front of the computer, working under the guise of researching a possible vacation but actually looking at…something else. And in the hall closet on the second floor, sparks had rained, spraying onto the summer clothes and storage boxes, igniting cloth and cardboard. By the time they were aware of the fire, all they had time to do was rescue Kathy.

Elliot had been in jeans and a sweatshirt, Faye in the flannel nightgown she'd received for Christmas two weeks earlier, Kathy wrapped in her crib's blankets. They went outside in the brisk January air, Elliot calling 911 on his way out. And then they watched.

Had it only been his family who'd watched, Elliot had thought, it would've been all right. Well, not all right, but bearable. But it hadn't just been his family watching their dreams burn, it'd been the entire neighborhood. His neighbors watching his house burn was what Elliot remembered most about that night. Elliot despised those people. They'd been the first people Elliot saw every morning when he awoke just before his eyes opened.

He lived in a one-bedroom apartment in the middle of the

city now. He'd moved there after Faye had filed for divorce last year. *Let it go,* she'd said. But he couldn't. He couldn't erase the memories of the onlookers watching his house burn as though it were entertainment. For them, it had been entertainment. When the roof had collapsed, a few young men from around the block—one of them Tommy Hutchinson, their paperboy—gasped, smiling, as though they had just witnessed the largest, brightest of all firework explosions. Elliot remembered the almost erotic look on his neighbors' faces because something was happening in *their* neighborhood. Even the local TV news reporter covered the fire like a circus. Fuck Must See TV.

How could Elliot forget it?

How could he forgive it?

He couldn't. Someone had to be held accountable. The fire had been damaging enough but to have been paraded out there, watched like lab animals, the onlookers waiting for their reactions; shown on the news at 5:30 AM, 6 AM, 6:30 AM, and several morning updates during the morning shows, the noon newscast, the 5 PM, 5:30 PM, 6 PM, and, of course, the 11:00 nightly news. The same video loop:

CLOSE-UP: Elliot standing, watching his life burn to ashes.

CUT TO: Faye holding Kathy, crying.

CLOSE-UP: goddamnit, of Kathy.

CUT TO: The roof caving in amid the flames.

INTERCUT: Reactions from neighbors who were on the scene, those media whores who looked oh-so-solemn onscreen, playing the role of their lives, greedily accepting Warhol's fifteen minutes—or seconds in the digital age; a soundbyte.

Elliot played all this back as he sat in his car, the last string to his past, and watched Tommy Hutchinson—now going by Tom because he was a star high school athlete, no longer a paperboy. Tom leaned against his car, a red colored Ford Mustang, smiling and laughing with a few more jocks, his red and white letter jacket bright on the cold, gray day.

Just let it go, Faye had said. After the investigation had proved faulty wiring had caused the fire, after the insurance money came through, after the settlement with the electrician, they'd bought a new house. But Elliot hadn't been able to let it go. How could he trust *these* neighbors? How would he know that *these* people weren't media whores waiting for something bad to happen to him? Elliot didn't know. There was only one way to find out and he'd be damned if he'd allow himself and his family to be paraded in front of his neighbors and the world again.

He couldn't trust his coworkers at the office, either. The way the other accountants had whispered behind his back. The way they'd avoided him. They couldn't have been trusted. They just couldn't. Finally, his manager had asked to see him. Told him he had to *let it go*. That's all anyone wanted from Elliot: for him to *let it go*.

His career was ruined. His marriage, ruined. His life, ruined. Because of the fire. Because of the onlookers. They were willing to help *after* the fire. *If you need anything...*, they'd said. *If you need anything....*

That was after the fire. But *during* the fire? During the fire: nothing. Not even a glass of water to throw on the burning house. Why would they want to help? Free entertainment doesn't come along often.

Elliot blinked back to the current when the red and white letter jacket moved and Tom Hutchinson got into his car, smiling and waving to his friends. If today was like any other day, Tom would be driving through Clifford and on Turner Road, around the dangerous Turner Bends, where more than one driver had met their fate.

The first snowflakes were beginning to fall.

Tom had been a good kid, or so Elliot had thought before the fire. Three years later he seemed to be doing well. Tom worked at the Turner Country Club on Turner Road, about half a mile from the Bends. He worked Tuesdays, Wednesdays, and Thursdays, game time permitting. It was probably some grunt job, washing dishes or something, but a job was a job and at least the young man worked, though it would turn out to be his undoing.

Word was he'd been offered a football scholarship from UMass. Maybe even URI. Maybe even further up the higher education echelon. Young, good looking, drove a nice car; you had to hand it to Tom, he had the life. Elliot was somewhat jealous just because of that. But the little bastard and his friends had watched and laughed while Elliot's house had burned, the media-desensitized little fuckers.

Elliot followed Tom. Tom was the typical high school jock. Drove fast. Too fast. Elliot drove faster than he usually did just to keep up. They turned onto Route 6 just as they had so many times before and stopped for a red light at the intersection with Turner Road.

Today would be the day. Elliot was sure of it.

After the lights, Turner Road went straight for half a mile before a minor bend and then another minor bend. Then there'd be a patch of ruler-straight road followed by the infamous Turner Bends, four dangerous curves like a two S's fused together at the tail of one and the crown the other. Elliot sped up. He approached Tom's car, Massachusetts license plate number STREAK, Tom's nickname on the field. A little tap was all it would take. They rounded the first bend. Snowflakes came at the windshield in streaks. They rounded the second bend. The third bend. Tom drove much too fast over here. Could he have been aware of Elliot following him? No, Elliot decided. Tom was too busy being Tom Hutchinson to notice anything outside his personal sphere of consciousness.

On the fourth and final Turner Bend, Elliot went too far out and crossed the yellow line. It was only a moment. A school bus headed right for him, its headlights on. Elliot wrenched the steering wheel to the left, pulling too hard, and his Toyota Camry shot too far over, hit a dirt patch, and spun.

The car came to a stop in a cloud of dust, facing the wrong way. Somehow, he hadn't hit any of the trees. Somehow, he'd hit no cars. Somehow, Elliot lived to try again tomorrow, a Thursday. Tom Hutchinson's death *had* to look like an accident. Because two murders in the same neighborhood would raise suspicions.

Manny Sylvia had lived across the street from the Marshalls the entire time they'd lived on Thoreau Street. A loud man who spent most summers outside without a shirt on, cooking on the grill and mowing the lawn.

He'd been the first one in front of the TV cameras. Elliot had taken note of that. He'd also been the only one to bring out a bottle of beer to watch the fire, like it was one of the sporting events Manny talked about so goddamn much. Manny was one of those guys who thought *every* guy liked the three B's: baseball (which symbolized all sports), beer, and boobs. Manny's wife had left some time ago. That was fine with him, a man liked to have a house to himself sometimes. Didn't have to worry about putting down the toilet seat.

Elliot parked two streets over on Emerson Street. He walked to Thoreau Street, a gloved hand in his coat holding the hard metal. It was a little past one in the morning and no one was out. This area was dead at this time of night. Unless someone's home was burning down, Elliot reminded himself. Then it was like Mardi Gras.

Elliot walked down the street, passing the familiar houses, heart ramming. God, he missed this neighborhood. God, he was glad he wasn't here anymore now that he knew how the people who lived in the neighborhood really were. Elliot stopped in front of where his house once stood.

A new house had been built in the last three years. The house was a cookie-cutter-quickie, nothing to distinguish it from any of the other houses on the street. The only thing remaining on the lot that indicated Elliot Marshall had ever lived here, had ever made his home here, was the cherry tree he'd planted when Kathy had been born. His heart reached for the tree, wanting to touch it as though physical contact would take him back to a happier time.

He turned away from the house and toward Manny Sylvia's house, squeezing his eyes shut to stop any unwanted tears. He reminded himself to stay focused on the task at hand.

At a backyard barbecue Elliot had been cajoled into attending (this had been when Manny was still married and Faye had been friendly with Mrs. Sylvia), Manny had told how he always kept a key to the house on the outside doorjamb for those nights he'd been brought home after his keys had been taken away.

When Manny had been at work two days ago, Elliot found the key in that spot, even after all these years. The security code had been easy enough to figure out: the number of the house. And since Manny was a Real Man, it didn't take Elliot long to find the first gun. Manny owned six guns in all, four handguns and two rifles, including an AR-15. Elliot knew nothing about guns and thought they should be outlawed because of the exact sort of thing he was doing.

Elliot had taken the key and a gun. He now returned to Manny Sylvia's house with one thing on his mind. He let himself in and punched in the security code. The image of Manny watching Elliot's house burn, sipping beer, crept into his head and convinced him this was the right thing.

Elliot quietly climbed the stairs to the second floor and peeked inside the bedroom. Manny lay on the bed, snoring, Fox News on the TV across the room. Elliot put the gun against Manny's head. If anyone heard the report, no one would do anything about it, blaming those goddamn kids and their firecrackers. Holdovers from New Years, perhaps.

There was movement behind Elliot and he turned. A woman he hadn't known was in the house stood there, mouth agape. She was dressed in sweatpants and a coat, her gloves still in her hands and her cheeks still red from the cold outside. It was Elizabeth Hanson from next door. Elliot had always suspected she and Manny were fucking around. He wondered if Elizabeth's husband, Rex, had any inkling.

"Ell—" was all she was able to say when Elliot turned the gun on her and fired.

He'd been three feet away from her and the bullet went through her face, snapping her head back, and she stumbled into the hallway.

Manny groaned and began to wake. Luckily, he was drunk. Had he been sober, he probably would've snapped awake and wrestled Elliot to the floor. Probably still would if he realized what was happening. Elliot would be no match for Manny. But Manny had drunk himself to a state where sleep wouldn't release its hold on him quickly enough and Elliot went with his original plan: he put the barrel of the pistol against Manny's right temple and squeezed the trigger. Then he fixed Manny's hand around the gun and left. Elliot had worn gloves the whole time and had kept his hair under a hat. He wasn't concerned with being caught.

Back at the car on Emerson Street, Elliot took in a deep (albeit shaky) breath of fresh air, started the car, and drove away.

The phone rang at 6:45 the next morning, waking Elliot.

"Where were you last night?" Faye asked. She sounded alert, her voice urgent, not her usual mornings-are-not-my-forte self.

"Here," he said. "I fell asleep watching a movie I rented. Why?"

There was a long pause as though Faye was considering something. He supposed she was. He couldn't stop himself, however, from being a little hurt.

"I...um...." Faye hesitated. Elliot wondered if she would come right out and admit her suspicions. "I just found out Manny Sylvia and Elizabeth Hanson were murdered last night. I wondered if you'd heard."

"Oh, shit," Elliot said, surprised by the genuine shock in his voice. "Is Rex okay?"

"I don't know, I didn't talk to—Wait. You mean was he...?"

"Yeah," he said hoping he hadn't put too much emphasis in it.

"Oh. No. Elizabeth and Manny were...."

"Oh," Elliot said. "I always thought the two of them were awfully close."

"Yeah," Faye said.

The few moments of silence that followed were almost unbearable. Elliot thought he heard Faye trying to articulate something but couldn't be sure. He remembered the smell of her hair as they lay in bed together in those few moments of silence right after they'd checked on Kathy and before their nighttime chit-chatter. Elliot closed his eyes against the memories. With the phantom smell of Faye's hair, the phantom smell of burning wood eventually followed.

"Well," Faye said. "I know you have a hard day ahead of you and I do too, so goodbye. You're still coming for Kathy on Saturday, right?"

"Wouldn't miss it," Elliot said.

They said goodbye and hung up. He'd had it on the tip of his tongue, he was sure Faye had it on the tip of hers. Three lousy words, three lousy syllables. But he couldn't say them. Not yet.

He turned on the news and caught the tail end of the upcoming news stories for later in the day. They showed the white medical examiner van in front of Manny Sylvia's house. They showed a stretcher being wheeled away from the house, a covered body on the stretcher, and then the news anchor was back promising more later, to have a good day.

The stretcher with a white sheet. The human shape under the sheet.

It hit Elliot hard and his stomach flopped. His heart stopped. He ran to the bathroom and opened the toilet lid just in time. After vomiting, he went back to the living room and sat staring at the TV, not paying attention to the morning show people discussing the overnight news.

He'd crossed the line. He'd crossed the line between man and animal. Somehow, he'd allowed himself to spiral into the cesspool of human emotions and be enveloped by rage and hatred. He'd always considered himself an intellectual, prided himself on thinking before reacting, measuring out his responses. Yet, here he'd allowed the feelings within to grow and turn sour over three years until it had become too goddamn much. Then he'd snapped, resulting with two dead people. People he'd known. People who'd once been neighbors, acquaintances if not quite friends, people to whom you'd go to borrow a cup of flour, people who'd invited him to neighborhood barbecues, people who'd stood outside that night in early January three years ago watching as his house, his dreams, burned to the ground like it was some spectator sport or movie, and even though they'd offered help afterward, even though they'd offered support, it hadn't been real, just a game just a fucking part they were supposed to play for the cameras those motherfucking cameras and the news reporter and themselves and to fuck with the Marshalls wasn't it a good show last night? wasn't it just spectacular the way the flames went so high? and Elliot remembered Elizabeth Hanson's husband, Rex, outside with a *video camera* and—

Elliot threw the remote control across the room. It smashed

into the faux wood paneling and broke, spewing batteries and circuit boards. A moment later there was a thump on the wall from the person who lived in the apartment next door. Elliot didn't respond. He stayed on the couch, staring at the TV without seeing it.

He'd been upset for a moment because he'd crossed the line from human to animal. He shook his head. Mankind crossed that line a long time ago. He was going with the flow.

Elliot opened a shade to a slate gray sky. He didn't need to go outside to smell the snow in the air. The other day hadn't been much more than flurries. Today, though, would be worse.

By one o'clock, snowflakes fell rapidly from the sky. Elliot sat in front of Clifford High waiting to see if the students would be released early. Fifty minutes later, a buzzing was heard from across campus. A few minutes after that, the first in a sea of students came through the doors. Elliot sat and waited for Tom Hutchinson, staring at the young man's Mustang.

Tom eventually came out with a girl. They weren't holding hands and their body language seemed to suggest they were flirting a little, testing the waters. The girl, an attractive blonde with long hair and a nice smile, seemed to like Tom. Tom walked straight and self-assured. His smile never faltered and he never seemed to be at a loss for words. Completely opposite from what Elliot had gone through in high school. Just another reason.

Then a thought came to Elliot that made his blood run cold and he sat straighter in his seat. What if this girl was going with Tom? What if Tom had called the country club and had found out he needn't bother going to work tonight because the snow was too bad? What if Tom and the girl were going to go to one of their houses? Elliot didn't want to cause harm to an innocent person. Killing those who'd wronged him was one thing, killing someone who didn't know him just because she associated with a person who'd wronged him was insane. Elliot barely felt the pain in his hands from clutching the steering wheel. He sat straight and watched.

Tom and the girl had stopped a few feet from Tom's car.

They talked, smiling. Then the girl said something that made Tom smile broader, and they said goodbye. The girl's car, a light green Volkswagen Beetle, was parked near Tom's Mustang and Elliot realized Tom had probably planned it this way, the conniving motherfucker. Tom watched the girl get into her car and start it, then he raised a hand as she backed out of her space and drove away. He got into his car, started it, gunned it, then pulled out too fast and took off even faster.

Elliot followed.

The wet, heavy snow didn't deter Tom from driving too fast, though he drove slower than he would have on dry land. In turn, Elliot drove much faster than he was comfortable with in this weather and this added to the adrenaline that already flowed through his bloodstream. And then the unthinkable happened. The traffic lights at the intersection of Route 6 and Turner Road went red and Tom sped up and ran the light! Elliot hadn't anticipated such a reckless, stupid act and stopped short, causing the car to weave on the slippery road.

Cars beeped on Route 6 but the lights hadn't changed right away, a delay system to keep light-runners from killing people, Elliot assumed. The light was a long one and when it finally turned green, Elliot moved forward slowly, trying not to get stuck. Elliot figured Tom was probably already at the country club, assuming he hadn't crashed into a tree or another car on the Bends.

He'd wait. He hadn't wanted to wait until the end of Tom's shift because he already felt he had pushed his luck by following Tom as much as he had but he also wanted to move on. There were at least five more former neighbors that needed to be taught a lesson, and then there was the reporter who'd covered the fire. Elliot was a busy man and Time waits for no one. Tom Hutchinson was going to die today.

Waiting would probably work out better, anyway, Elliot decided. Although the roads were slippery now with the snow having fallen for two hours, by the time Tom left the club the snow will have really made a mess of things and an accident would be more likely. And easier to pull off. Besides, Elliot wouldn't have to rush along behind Tom right now. He could focus on the dangerously slick road.

He came to the bends and slowed to just above twenty miles an hour. He took the first bend and felt the back wheels slide just a bit. He brought the car down to fifteen and made the second bend. He was on the third bend when headlights came around from the opposite direction. The car was going too fast and slid. It smashed into Elliot, hard. Glass broke as the whole front of his car was pushed back on him. The airbag inflated, blocking Elliot's sight. His right leg exploded in pain as it snapped, covering the pain he felt in his left wrist. The world went gray as the car hit a tree and slid off the road, turning over. Then the world went black.

It was strange how the world worked sometimes, how Fate liked to fuck with people. When Elliot woke up in the hospital, he found a plethora of injuries had happened to him: broken leg and wrist, a concussion, fractured ribs, and some internal bleeding. But he would pull through. Not the driver of the other car, though. A kid who'd gone to work and found out he wasn't needed and that they'd forgotten to call him. A kid who then got into his Ford Mustang and left, driving too fast on Turner Road, ignorant of the dangers of the slick road and the Bends. The kid had died. They wouldn't say much else, they being the officials, the authorities. It was Faye who informed him, teary-eyed, that it had been Tommy Hutchinson, their old paperboy on Thoreau Street, who'd been driving the other car that had almost killed him. Then Faye kissed his forehead before she left and promised to return. Elliot smiled and nodded.

Maybe it was time to let it go, he thought. Maybe what had happened to him had been a sign. Maybe his life hadn't been destroyed after all but, instead, a new one had begun. Elliot felt better than he had in almost three years. His mission was done, he decided.

He turned on the TV to the local news. There was a house fire in New Bedford and a reporter was talking to an eyewitness. Elliot recognized the reporter. Maybe there was one more person he needed to visit after all, he thought, before he let it go.

SNOW DAY

Missy woke up excited. The Peter Rabbit clock on the wall said it was past the time she normally woke up for school. The wind outside howled and moaned and, thinking about the night before when the snowstorm began, Missy jumped out of bed. Giant snowflakes streamed past her window.

"Cool," she said.

Missy threw on longjohns, jeans, a turtleneck shirt, and a sweater. She brushed her teeth and brushed out her long, raven black hair. On the kitchen table was a note her mother had left before going to work.

Missy—
No school today! You can go outside
but STAY NEAR THE BUILDING. And try
to be with a friend. Things are SCARY.
Love,
Mommy

Missy wolfed down a bowl of Count Chocula cereal and threw on her snowboots and coat.

Things are SCARY. Mommy had been talking about the baby who'd gone missing from the lady on the first floor yesterday. The police had been at their apartment building and everything last night, asking everyone if they'd seen anything. Of course, no one had.

"If we didn't need the money," Mommy had said between cigarette puffs, looking at the snow beginning to fall. "I'd stay home with you tomorrow."

Missy called Kathy Chambers, her best friend, and told

Kathy she'd meet her at the outside back door. A few minutes later, they met.

"Did the police talk to you?" Kathy asked.

"Yeah," Missy said. "They asked if I'd seen anyone suspicious around the building."

"What did you say?"

"I told them the truth." Missy tried catching a snowflake on her tongue. "I said no. What about you?"

"Daddy wouldn't let them talk to me." Kathy studied random snowflakes on her mittens. "He said they might frighten me. He lied and said I wasn't outside all day because I was punished."

"The cops believed him?"

"Yeah," Kathy said. "He was drunk."

Missy nodded as if that explained everything. They worked together to push open the back door against a snowdrift. Wind slashed at their faces as they walked through the snow, into the small yard. The snow was six inches high and counting.

"Whattaya wanna do?" Kathy asked.

"I dunno," Missy said. "Wanna play house? We can pretend we're Eskimos or something."

"Okay."

They trundled through the snow and howling, biting wind. A wooden fence across from the building blocked off a vacant lot. Missy tried to push a loose plank out of the way.

"Help me," she grunted. "The snow's making this hard."

Kathy helped Missy push the plank open and they squeezed into the vacant lot.

Snow covered old, abandoned furniture and trash. The girls went to a shed and opened the door. Peeling blood red paint sprinkled on the virgin white snow.

"The wind sounds funny here," Kathy said.

"That's 'cause it's between buildings," Missy said.

"I know. It still sounds funny. Like people crying."

"You're weird."

Missy pushed aside an old, rusted trashcan.

"Is it still there?" Kathy asked.

"Yep," Missy said and pulled out a black garbage bag.

"I wanna be the mommy," Kathy said. "You were the mommy yesterday."

"Okay," Missy said and pulled out the little baby they'd stolen from the lady on the first floor.

The baby had turned blue overnight, his eyes had frosted white, and icicles hung from his chin and nose.

"Keep your gloves on," Missy said. "I saw someone on TV go to jail because they left fingerprints."

"'Kay," said Kathy.

And the girls began playing house.

THE UMBRELLA PEOPLE

Gerard chuckled when he saw the man with the gray trench coat and fedora holding an open black umbrella. It was one of those moments that should've disappeared as quickly as the sound of that chuckle, Gerard later thought. The early June sun fell on New Bedford without intensity but keeping the coastal city warm. The streets of downtown held an unusual amount of smiling people, many colors of clothing, and the feeling that summer was here and the cold, hard reality of the world could be left behind for a season. And amongst it all was this man dressed for a rainy October day.

Gerard returned his attention to driving and trying to find a song on the radio that he could listen to, enjoy, but not be assaulted by bad music or bad vocals. That ruled out almost everything. The umbrella man was gone from his mind.

It wasn't until the end of the afternoon as he boarded the elevator with Harris Jones, both ready to start the weekend, that the umbrella man came back to him.

"You won't believe what I saw at lunch," Harris said, loosening his tie and holding his suit jacket behind him.

"The city council in an orgy with goats?" Gerard said.

Harris laughed. "Sooner or later it'll be on public access. Seriously, though, at lunch I'm at the sandwich shop on Union Street and this guy walks by—"

"Amazing."

"Shut up. This guy walks by wearing a fuckin' *trench coat* and one of those Indiana Jones hats—"

"A fedora."

"—yeah, one of those—and he's holding an—"

"—open umbrella," Gerard finished. "Yeah, I saw him this morning on my way to work."

"Isn't that a fuckin' riot?" Harris said. He only cursed that much on Friday afternoons. "One of the most beautiful days of the year and some psycho's dressed for a goddamn monsoon."

The elevator doors opened to the garage and the coworkers stepped out.

"Only in fuckin' New Bedford, man," Harris said.

Gerard smiled and fought the urge to point out that strange people populate every city. Doomsayers with sandwich boards proliferate New York, weirdoes in Boston and L.A. Even small cities in southeastern Massachusetts like New Bedford and Fall River have them. He could point that out, but why bother? What good would it do?

"See ya Monday," Harris called as he climbed into his car.

Gerard waved. He soon drove toward the garage's exit ramp and as the gate rolled up, its clattering amplified to a roar in the tunnel, the umbrella man walked in front of the car and stopped. Gerard blinked, surprised at seeing him again, especially after talking to Harris about him only a few minutes ago. The man didn't look at Gerard but stared straight ahead, seemingly unaware of the car waiting to leave. The gate was rolled all the way up. The man didn't move. Gerard beeped.

The Umbrella Man slowly turned his head, revealing light blue eyes that were so bloodshot they appeared red. His cracked and peeling lips opened, revealing gray and black teeth.

"The storm's coming," he rasped.

Gerard blinked. He shouldn't have been able to hear the voice at all yet it sounded as though the man were in the car with him.

A horn blared behind Gerard and Harris shouted, "Move, ya fuckin' psycho!"

The Umbrella Man smiled and continued walking, destination unknown. Gerard pulled out of the garage and looked in the direction the man had gone. He just caught a glimpse of the black umbrella as it passed behind the corner of the building. Gerard shivered despite the warm air, and drove away.

He tried to have a good weekend, but he kept thinking of

the Umbrella Man and his storm. It frightened him, and the fright left him embarrassed.

On Sunday it was a woman wearing a dull cranberry trench coat, a rain bonnet, and holding a dirty yellow umbrella. Gerard was jogging, wearing shorts and an old, thin tee shirt. The sight of the woman stopped him. He was already breathing heavy and his heart beat a good Latin rhythm, but the cold that filled his chest was a direct result of the woman. She was across the street, in front of the vocational technical high school, and walking in the direction opposite from where Gerard was running. She looked at him without stopping and smiled.

"There's a storm coming," she said.

Her voice traveled across the busy boulevard to him. His feet froze. He actually stopped breathing he was so scared. The woman kept walking, not looking at him anymore, acting as though the world around her didn't exist, caught in her own, private storm.

Gerard watched the woman walk until she was out of sight. He didn't feel like jogging anymore that day. He walked home with questions running through his head. Was there a new cult? That was a little ridiculous, Gerard thought. He'd seen two people with umbrellas, dressed for rain on gorgeous sunny days, but only two. Two people hardly constituted a cult. It was more likely just odd occurrences in odd times.

At home, after his shower, Gerard tried to put the Umbrella People out of his mind. It hardly worked. He didn't know why these two people had disturbed him so much—

Maybe it's the fact that both sounded as though they were in your head, a voice suggested.

—but they did. Feelings, emotions, often had no basis in logic. Maybe these two people both had that condition that prohibited them from being in direct sunlight and that was how they protected themselves. No matter, they shouldn't have bothered him.

However, a little after eight that night, Gerard caught himself going through his apartment, looking out the windows, fearful he'd find Umbrella People walking up the street. His cheeks burned and he walked away from the window. He spent the rest of the night resisting the urge to keep checking. Later, as he drifted off to sleep, he laughed at himself.

You're like a cheesy 1950s sci-fi flick. Attack of the Umbrella People *or something.*

Somehow, the fully formed thought didn't seem as funny.

In the Monday morning light, the whole idea of Umbrella People scaring him seemed absurd. That didn't stop him from noting that he hadn't seen any of them on his drive downtown. He despised himself for feeling relieved by that.

In his cubicle, he let out a breath he hadn't realized he'd held. His hands trembled and he felt even more foolish. Harris erupted through the cubicle's opening and Gerard jumped, gasping.

"You are not going to believe this," Harris said. Though he smiled, it felt false. Gerard wasn't sure if he was projecting his own feelings onto Harris, but it seemed like his coworker had a nervous edge to him.

"Believe what?" Gerard asked, though he didn't think he really wanted to know.

"I'm dating this chick lives in Rochester, right? You familiar with the area?"

"Kinda."

"Well, there's this large white strip mall, nice looking place, has a deli, video store, small used bookstore."

"Yeah," Gerard said. "I've been to the bookstore."

"Well, there's this pizza place there. The chick I'm dating and I went there Saturday night, we were gonna have a pizza and rent a video. Well, I'm sitting in the place, small place with okay food, and looking out the window. You remember Saturday night, right? Warm, the sun was out till late."

"Gorgeous night," Gerard said, his voice low. He knew where the conversation was headed and didn't like it.

"Exactly. Gorgeous. Anyway, I'm sitting there biting into my linguica pizza when I see some yahoo walking through the parking lot. He's dressed normal except for a goddamn *umbrella.* Just like that whacko we saw Friday."

"Did he say anything to you?"

Harris blinked. He gulped. The smile remained on his face only now Gerard *knew* it was forced.

"Of course not," Harris said, a quiver in his voice. "He was outside and I was inside."

Gerard didn't believe him, not at all, but he nodded.

"I saw a woman with an umbrella Sunday morning while I was out jogging."

"Allison, the chick I'm dating, said she'd seen some, too."

"You told her about—?"

"No! And let her think I was a fuckin' basket case? She saw me looking at the man and she turned and looked. She said she saw a guy like that last week, with an umbrella and shit, from the bookstore where she works. On the fuckin' *Cape*."

The Umbrella People had already invaded Cape Cod and Rochester, a suburban area. It wasn't only a few nuts in the city anymore. And if they were in southeastern Massachusetts, why wouldn't they be elsewhere? How many Umbrella People were there in the whole Northeast? On the East Coast? Maybe the whole country was affected.

Stop it, he told himself. *This is crazy.*

"I don't know what's going on," Harris said. "But I'm going to find out."

"Just be careful." The warning surprised Gerard as much as it seemed to surprise Harris. Harris stared at him for several moments, he didn't seem to know what to do. Finally, he turned and left Gerard's cubicle.

Gerard went through the rest of the workday with growing apprehension. He found himself sneaking peeks out the windows whenever he passed one, looking at the street and at the people, waiting to see an umbrella amongst the moving heads, a blot on an otherwise colorful, varied collection. He saw none. He skipped lunch, convincing himself he had too much work to do. Actually, he thought he'd seen movement from Harris's cubicle during lunch but wasn't sure. Leaving work for the day was stressful; he and Harris barely spoke in the elevator. In his car, Gerard's hands ached from clutching the steering wheel with white-knuckled apprehension. But there was no Umbrella

Man, no Umbrella Woman, no Umbrella People. Not down-town, not in the north end.

Harris wasn't at work Tuesday.

Gerard didn't see any Umbrella People. Maybe it was over.

Wednesday. Gerard saw four different Umbrella People on his way to work. If he'd seen four, how many hadn't he seen? His heart rammed by the time he parked in the parking garage below the building. Sweat trickled down his face despite the air conditioning. He got to his cubicle as quickly as he could and sat, out of breath.

"This is fucking insane," he whispered. "Get a hold of yourself."

He forced himself to work. A little past 8:30, the phone rang.

"Gerard," Harris said when Gerard answered. "I under-stand now."

It took a few moments for him to find the words and he already knew what the answer was before he spoke them. But he couldn't not ask. "Understand what?"

"I under*stand*," Harris said. "I really do. There's a storm coming, Gerard. Just like they've said. A storm's co—"

Gerard hung up. He stood and left his cubicle. He didn't know where to go. He decided on Harris's cubicle. Once there, he turned on the computer and waited. Once the computer had booted up, he went online and checked Harris's browser history. Gerard didn't think during this time. Thinking would only try to rationalize the irrational. Luckily, Monday's his-tory was still available. Several Google searches had been performed.

Gerard gulped. *Umbrella* and *people* were the connecting words in these searches.

Gerard turned off the computer and left Harris's cubicle. Then he grabbed his stuff, told his supervisor he was taking a sick day, and left before he was asked anything.

As he pulled out of the garage, a man with an umbrella approached the car.

"It's coming, Gerard," Harris said. He hadn't shaven in two

days and his bloodshot eyes carried dark bags. "The storm's coming. Join us and you'll be safe."

Gerard had never burned rubber in his life. He didn't know he knew how until that moment, screeching away from the office building with Harris holding an umbrella over his head, shouting that a storm was coming.

Under the harsh sunlight on the way home he noticed a dozen or so Umbrella People. He got home and saw one standing on the corner of an intersection near his apartment house. She looked at Gerard, deep brown eyes taking him in, ebony skin glistening from the heat of the raincoat she wore.

"A storm is on the way," she said. It sounded like she said it in his ear.

Gerard sprinted to the door, let himself in, and ran up to the third floor. His hand shook so bad he had a hard time getting the key into the lock. Finally, he got the door open and entered, locking and chaining the door. Sweat dripped off his face and he pulled off his dress shirt, leaving his sweat-soaked undershirt, and pulled off his pants. Jeans got thrown on and throughout, Gerard tried to convince himself not to look outside.

It was futile.

There were two Umbrella People outside now: the Black woman and another woman, an older Latin American woman. Both clutched their umbrellas. Both stared up at Gerard.

He closed the blinds and stepped back. The cops. As crazy as it would sound to them, he had to try. Gerard picked up the phone and was about to dial the local number—not 911—when he heard static coming from the phone. Only, it wasn't static. His heart sank and his stomach tightened. The hairs on the back of his neck bristled. The sound of pouring, driving rain came from the phone. He listened, mesmerized by the sound. A crash came then and he hollered, dropping the phone. Thunder.

Get out of here, he told himself. *Grab some shit and hightail it outta here!*

He grabbed his backpack and threw some underwear, jeans, tee shirts, and a jacket in. Out of habit, he grabbed a book. He also took all the money he could find. A baseball cap on, he had one hand on the doorknob and the other ready to unchain the door when he heard something rustle on the other side.

Gerard stopped. His breath was the only sound in the apartment. He put an ear against the door. Nothing. Then the swoosh-click of an umbrella opening.

His hands dropped from the door and he stepped back. Footsteps went downstairs and the back door opened, then closed.

Mouth dry, Gerard went to the living room. Out the window, on the street below, what had to be close to one hundred Umbrella People mulled about. Together, their umbrellas formed a canopy that blocked his view of the ground. Many of them looked up in unison, looked *right at him*. Their eyes were all dull. No expression crossed their faces. Harris was one of them. Even with the window closed and the air conditioner running, Gerard heard them warning him of the coming storm. It wasn't a roar of voices one might get at a rock concert when everyone sings to their favorite songs, but a hundred voices speaking independently.

He closed the blind. He didn't believe in God. Now he wished he could.

The TV didn't help. Reports from around the country came in of people lining the streets, holding umbrellas. In some places, the army was called in. Video came of armed soldiers confronting a stoic mass of Umbrella People.

Gerard watched the news. Around quarter to seven that night, a special report interrupted the news about the Umbrella People. The news anchor looked grim.

Gerard turned the TV off. He didn't need to see the special report. He knew what it would be.

There was a storm coming.

STRAY CATS

Justin had begun dozing when the woman screamed, jarring him awake and alert in the rocking chair. It was almost one in the morning. He bent toward the open window.

The scream was as raw and primal as the sound of cats fighting. The woman's voice mixed fear and pain into a horrible crescendo. Goosebumps prickled over his body and ice filled his veins.

Justin saw two figures on a porch across the street and four houses down. He recognized Alice Lorenzo, the old woman who lived in the first floor apartment. He thought of her as the Cat Lady because she fed the neighborhood strays.

The second shape was of a man he didn't recognize. Big guy. Solid. A football player at some point or another, no doubt. The two silhouettes struggled. Then the Cat Lady's body jerked against the man's several times and finally fell to the porch.

Justin tried to move, tried to scream. He had to do something—anything—but was frozen.

The man turned from the Cat Lady and jumped off the porch, skipping the steps entirely. He ran down the street, away from Justin's window and toward the Avenue, where he disappeared, embraced by night shadows.

Gifford Street looked yellow under the street lamps. Until the moment the Cat Lady screamed, most of the lights in the two- and three-decker apartment houses lining the street had been off, the only sign of life the occasional car that went up the street from the Avenue to the Boulevard. Now lights came on in windows around the neighborhood.

Sirens approached from the distance and Justin found he

was able to move again. His heart rammed against his ribcage and he trembled.

A police car stopped in front of the Cat Lady's house. People came from their homes now, and, in a matter of seconds, four more squad cars and an ambulance arrived.

Claustrophobia struck Justin. The living room seemed too small, no larger than a broom closet. He could've done something to stop the attack. Could've run out of the apartment, could've screamed, could've fucking done *something* and yet....

A moment later he stood on the downstairs front porch, took a deep breath, and then started toward the crime scene. He didn't want to go, didn't want to be as obnoxious as some of his neighbors, who had to be told to stay behind the yellow police tape, but he knew he had to talk to the police.

Just don't look at the body, he told himself. He'd already seen more than he wanted to tonight.

He stopped at the yellow police tape and watched the police and medical examiner do their jobs. He got the attention of one of the officers handling crowd control and told him he'd seen the murder. A few moments later, he was led under the yellow tape to an unmarked police car that had a blue globe in the windshield.

A detective asked questions. Justin answered what he could. It wasn't much, but it was more than they'd had.

The detective thanked Justin, gave him his card, and asked if he could stop by the downtown station in the morning to give a full statement. Justin agreed and returned to the other side of the yellow tape. Passing his neighbors, they glared at him as if *he'd* done something wrong.

As he approached the front porch of his apartment house, movement caught the corner of his eye. The black cat he called Blacky stood watching the action from the porch of the house across the street. Another black cat, this one with white chest and paws (whom he called Paws) sat on the sidewalk in front of Justin's house, staring. Another cat, an orange one who'd just started hanging around the neighborhood, came out from behind a shrub and sat next to Paws.

Six eyes reflected flashing blue, red, and white lights. The cats were still as statues.

There was commotion from the crime scene and Justin turned toward it. The medical examiner's van drove slowly up the street. He watched the van drive by and wished he'd gone outside, yelled out the window, *anything* to have helped the Cat Lady. He held back tears as the weight of the whole thing fell on him. When someone's life had been on the line, he'd failed to act. Here he was, a guy who'd grown up playing superheroes and Jedi Knights, who'd read and studied about the great heroes of mythology and folklore, and the one chance he had to truly act like a hero, he'd frozen up and watched as an old woman was murdered. With a trembling hand, he wiped his eyes.

The stray cats watched the medical examiner pass. Blacky stood and went down a few porch steps, following the white van with his eyes as Paws turned his head almost all the way around, watching.

The crowd began to disperse from the Cat Lady's house and the strays scattered, disappearing behind the same bushes and fences from which they'd emerged moments before. Blacky was the last to go. He turned and looked at Justin, making eye contact as though to say, "You could've done something," and was gone. A chill rattled Justin.

Just your imagination, he told himself. *Your emotions. The cat didn't really look at you.*

Unable to get the idea out of his head, unable to get the guilt out of his heart, he returned to the sanctuary of his apartment.

The next morning, Justin went to the police station and gave his statement. He then went to work, pushing hard on the plans he was designing for a store that was being built in the North End of Harden. After work, he noticed all of Gifford Street was solemn; the neighbors, when they saw each other, did little more than nod to one another. Tomorrow, though, the gossip would start.

That night, sleep once again evaded Justin. He sat in the rocking chair, facing the open window just as he had the night before, when a life was lost because of inaction. Because of fear. It was warmer than the previous night but still cool and he savored the chill in the breeze. It made him feel fresh and alert and sometimes drove back the disappointment he felt in himself. But the air also carried with it an intensity that knotted his stomach and made his hands tremble.

Nevertheless, he nodded off a little after twelve. He thought he'd blinked but when he reopened his eyes it was almost two-thirty. The air was cooler and the intensity was even thicker. The sound of a cat mewing rode the breeze through the screen, chilling him even more than the cold air it glided in on.

Justin leaned forward, pressed his forehead against the screen, and looked to the street below. Blacky sat on a porch across the street, his eyes more evident than his black body.

Meeerrrroowww.

The sound was long and haunting. He saw Paws and the new orange cat (who he'd started thinking of as Tropicana) slink over to Blacky. Upon seeing his two comrades, Blacky flowed down the porch steps and started down the street. Paws and Tropicana followed closely.

As Justin watched them he didn't want to believe it. Refused to believe it. Yet the feeling wouldn't leave him. So it came as no surprise when the three cats ended up on the Cat Lady's porch.

Meerrrooowww.

Yyarrroooowww.

Justin got up, threw on his sneakers and a jacket, and went outside. He was about to take the last step off the porch when a cat he'd never seen before streaked past him.

Cats, at least fifty of them, slinked down the street around him. Meows came from everywhere as they gathered around the Cat Lady's porch.

Staying on his side of the street, Justin continued until he stood directly across from the porch. He watched in disbelief and realized at that moment, if they really wanted to, they could kill him. He told himself—*screamed* at himself—to get home and go to bed.

But he couldn't. He tried to move but his feet just wouldn't budge. Just like last night.

Then Blacky, followed by Paws and Tropicana, slithered down the stairs and began slinking down the street, toward the Avenue. The other cats followed.

Transfixed, the invisible clamps that had held him in place released Justin and he followed them as well.

The cats mainly stuck to yards and shadows. Justin wasn't so fortunate, not being as quick, balanced, or graceful. He followed their sounds, sounds no one else seemed to notice. Then again, those who were out this late (or early) weren't listening for them.

The cats entered a well-lit alley behind a bar that acted like a last piece of a puzzle. It all fell together for Justin.

It was the Cat's Club, a strip club that had just barely been allowed to move in. Alice Lorenzo headed a local group that had almost succeeded in closing it down the year before. Mrs. Lorenzo had counseled a young woman who'd allegedly been raped by the bar's proprietor and had talked the young woman into speaking out at a city council meeting.

Behind the club, cats covered the blacktop, roofs, fences, a car, and a dumpster. All at once, they looked at him.

He knew what they wanted him to do.

He turned away from the alley and walked to the front of the building. The club had closed at two but for some reason the front door was still open.

An empty stage was the first thing he noticed as it took up more space than anything else. Tables were vacant and the bar was an empty way station on the landscape. Thankfully, no bouncers mulled around. Neither did anyone else. Unless they were in a back room, Justin was by himself.

A door behind the bar squealed open and a man who stood over six feet sauntered out cleaning a glass. Justin recognized him as the proprietor of the Cat's Club. And the man who had murdered Alice Lorenzo.

"We're closed," the man said.

Run, Justin's mind screamed at him. *Get the hell outta here and call the cops.*

Justin's feet became ice and his mouth went dry. Call the police. Sound advice.

"Sorry."

"Wait a sec," the man said, placing the glass down and playing with a keychain on his belt. "C'mon back and have a drink."

Justin nodded and moved to the bar. It was impossible for the man to know who he was, where he'd come from, or why he was there. He'd been four houses away, at night, behind a screen of a second floor window. Impossible for the man to know.

"I don't remember ever seeing you in here," the man said. The keychain was a pewter wolf's head.

"I happened to be in the neighborhood and was a little thirsty," Justin said.

"It's funny," the man said. "That a person would be passing by a closed bar after three in the morning and decide to drop in for a drink. Especially when it's someone who looks more ready for bed than a drink." He smiled. It wasn't pleasant. "A beer?"

Justin couldn't speak so nodded. He kept his hands under the bar afraid the man might see them trembling.

"You from around here?" the man asked as he poured a beer.

"A few streets away," Justin said and then froze.

What the fuck did you just do? he screamed at himself. He couldn't believe he'd let his autopilot carry him like that.

"You saw what happened last night," the man said. "Didn't you?" It was a vague question, could've been anything.

"What are you talking about?" Justin hoped he'd sounded convincing but was afraid his face had betrayed him.

"The fight," the man said. "One of the dancers and myself. You know, the argument. She wanted more money. You came tonight to make sure she was okay. I've seen it before."

Justin felt like a mountain was taken off him. "Yeah," he said. "That's it."

The man put both hands on the bar. The left one held a knife with a six-inch blade. "There was no argument last night," he said through his teeth. "But you saw something anyway."

There was a hiss as a black cat came from nowhere. It leapt at the man's face, scratching it. The man yelled and cursed as Justin started for the door. The man's arm shot out, grabbed him by the shoulder, and threw him into the stage.

Justin rolled onto it just as the man arced the knife down and into the floorboards, then Justin stood and ran behind the curtain.

Meeoow.

The sound came from his right, from an open door that led to a hallway. He went through just as the man slashed through the curtain.

"You fucker!" the man yelled.

The hallway was long. Light came from a doorway a few feet away. At the very end of it was an exit. Someone or something— a whole lot of somethings—rammed against it. The ramming on the exit door became louder and more intense the further down the hall Justin went.

The man lunged into the hallway from the stage area, knife glittering. Justin ran toward the exit but the man gained quickly.

Just as he reached the lighted room, the exit door crashed open. Stray cats flowed into the hallway like water into a cabin of a sinking ship.

Justin leapt into the room.

The strays ran by the door and a moment later the man screamed from the hallway.

Justin approached the open door. Cats streamed past, running through the hallway in a seemingly endless current. The killer lay on the floor with the cats running straight over him. Eventually they began to peter out and were soon gone, apparently using the front door to escape.

The man who'd killed Alice Lorenzo laid face down, blood pooling around him on the floor. When the cats had rushed him, he'd fallen on his own knife, the same knife that had killed Alice Lorenzo.

Still shaking, Justin slipped out the back door.

Blacky, Paws, and Tropicana were sitting in the alley waiting for him. Tropicana walked over to him, looked up, and then continued on her way. Paws rubbed against him, letting out a small meow, and followed the other cat. Blacky sat in the alley a moment longer, licking a paw. When he was done, he picked something up in his teeth and approached Justin. His eyes closed a little as he rubbed against him, and dropped what he'd been holding. He meowed, and then disappeared into the night. Justin knelt down and saw that Blacky had dropped the killer's pewter wolf's head keychain at his feet.

Justin took a final glance at the killer, closed the back door, and went home, leaving the keychain where it lay.

Justin began feeding the cats in the backyard so none of the neighbors would see. Every night, as he put the food bowl down, he felt like he was being watched. In the morning the food would be gone. The cats always came.

After all, it was their party, their neighborhood. He just lived there. They all just lived there.

OLD NELLY'S HIGH PRICE

Jimmy Block yelped and leapt away from the closet, instantly embarrassed. He'd worked for the Harden Housing Authority for twenty-five years and had seen a lot of strange shit working in the apartments, but what he saw in Old Nelly Janks's closet rivaled it all. Candles lined the perimeter on small tables and shelves. On what Jimmy decided must've been an altar laid a doll. It looked handmade, a voodoo doll. Underneath the altar were small vials and jars containing powders and liquids. Jimmy's first reaction to the vials was that Old Nelly was a drug dealer. But that wasn't right, not with all the other shit in the closet. Then his eyes fell on four jars underneath the altar. The contents of the jars looked like rotten fruit floating in yellowish juice, but when Jimmy put his glasses on and leaned closer, he saw they were really shrunken heads. Above all the strange shit was the water pipe Jimmy had been following.

His partner, Arnold, who'd worked for the Housing Authority about as long as Jimmy, rushed into the room. "You all right?"

Jimmy nodded toward the closet.

Arnold looked and smiled. "You didn't know Old Nelly's into black magic?"

Jimmy opened his mouth to respond when Old Nelly's scratchy voice came from behind.

"'tain't no such ting as 'black magic,'" she said. The small Black woman came in hunched over her cane, each step bringing a small gasp. She looked from Arnold to Jimmy, smiling mostly toothless and with no sign of humor. Jimmy had never seen the woman quite so serious before. "Dere's only *magic*. It's what people use it for dat makes it good or bad. Black or White."

Then she cackled, the Old Nelly Janks that Jimmy was used to was there again. "Don't know why black be bad, dough. I usually have more trouble wit Whites."

Jimmy's heart sank as he entered the apartment to the sound of Clarice's coughs. The coughs came from deep within her chest and tore through her lungs and throat. He waited for the cough to subside before going into the bedroom.

"Hey, baby."

"Hi, honey," Clarice said and stood to kiss him.

"How you feeling?"

"Eh-eh," she said, her flat hand seesawing. "How was your day?" Her voice was hoarse.

She's been coughing like that all day, Jimmy thought. *Again.*

"As good as it gets, I suppose."

"I haven't put the coffee on yet," Clarice said. "I'll go do it now."

"It's okay," Jimmy said. "Lay down. I'll worry about it. You wanna cup?"

"Tea wouldn't be bad," Clarice said, returning to bed.

Jimmy nodded and went into the kitchen, placing his small cooler on the table with his keys on the way, and turned on the range. The pilot was out, again. Grumbling, he lit it. Sometimes he thought that maybe they'd be better off living in the projects.

Back into the bedroom, Clarice had turned on the television and watched the last few minutes of Ellen DeGeneres. Jimmy sat beside her and ran a hand through her hair. He remembered when it had been dark brown and thick when they'd met thirty years ago. Now it was gray and thin. The dim light from the TV showed just how dark the bags under her eyes had become and Jimmy clung to the fading image of Clarice in her youth, before the chronic bronchitis and, eventually the—

No. He couldn't think about it. Better to think of other things.

"Is Pauline home?" he asked.

"Not yet," Clarice said.

Almost on cue, the back door opened and Pauline entered, softly reciting some rap song that had the words *bitch* and *sucker* and *motherfucker* as key components as she went the six inches from the backdoor to her bedroom. Her bedroom door closed and a moment of silence followed, shattered by a blast of pop music.

Jimmy stood, ready to tell her to keep her music down, but Clarice grabbed his forearm and stopped him. Her grip was weak, unable to hold on any tighter, but it was enough. Jimmy sat, looking at the floor.

"She's a teenager," Clarice said. A rattle at the back of her throat indicated a cough was building.

The whistle from the kitchen broke in and Clarice coughed. Just hearing the long whooping made Jimmy's chest ache. He stood and watched, hands out as if she was about to fall out of bed.

"I'm fine," Clarice said between coughs. "Go make..." Cough. "...the drinks."

Jimmy nodded.

The coughing faded as he walked away from their bedroom but his heart kept its steady rapping. They'd promised each other forever but it was too soon for forever to come. Pauline's bedroom door opened and the noise she called music flowed out. She came out, singing along.

"Hi," Jimmy said, trying not to bitch about her music.

"Hi," said Pauline and went to the refrigerator.

She looked inside and he glanced over at her. Her jeans were tight and had holes all over, the current fashion according to her. Her stomach showed beneath a crimson top that seemed to have melted onto her breasts. A gold ring looped out from her belly-button. Oh, the war that had taken place over that goddamn ring.

"Could you get me the milk, please?" he asked.

She looked at him from under the wavy strands of blonde hair, her mascara-lined blue eyes looking annoyed by his presence. He remembered those blue eyes when they'd been full of wonder, full of love. Pauline took the gallon from the top shelf and handed it to him.

"Thank you," he said. "How's your vacation?"

"It's okay."

He poured the milk into his coffee and Clarice's tea. "Keeping out of trouble?"

Pauline sighed and closed the refrigerator door. "What's that supposed to mean?"

Jimmy bit his inner cheek. "I don't know." *Don't do it*, he warned himself. *Don't start anything.* "Should it mean something?"

"There you go again," Pauline said. "You just think all I do is get into trouble."

"Tell me if you do anything else," Jimmy said and put the milk away. "I want to know what you do all day while your mother is sick."

"I was with Nigel today and—"

Jimmy had been reaching in the cabinet for the honey and glanced back at Pauline. "You're still with him? Why can't you find someone more...?"

"More what? More *white*?"

"No," Jimmy said but didn't sound convincing to his own ears. "Just someone with a better prospect. I mean, what's he do? Does he have a job? Does he—?"

"I'm pregnant!" Pauline yelled.

The two surprising words echoed through Jimmy's head. Pregnant. His little girl.

Clarice coughed from the bedroom, breaking the silence. Pauline rushed into her bedroom and slammed the door. Jimmy went into the kitchen to finish the drinks. Hands trembling, he put extra honey in Clarice's tea to cover up the salty tears that had fallen in.

After supper, Jimmy stood on the front porch, a can of Coors in his hand, looking down from their third floor apartment in the triple-decker house. The sun lowered in the western sky.

Jimmy saw himself as a pretty laid back guy but if he saw that nigger-spic, Nigel Sanchez, right now, he'd kill the fucker.

What the hell was Pauline trying to do? Kill Clarice? For God's sake, Clarice was dying. She didn't need knowing that their daughter had ruined her life.

Jimmy sipped his beer and silently wept.

"What's eating you?" Arnold asked the next day as they had lunch.

"Nothing," Jimmy said.

Arnold looked over at him from the passenger seat of the Housing Authority's pickup truck. "I know something's wrong, Jimmy. We've worked together too long for me not to."

"Pauline's pregnant." Jimmy did everything he could not to cry.

Arnold nodded. "She still going with that Black fella?"

"Black *and* Mexican," Jimmy said before he could stop himself. He looked at Arnold, hoping he hadn't offended him by the way he'd said it.

Arnold laughed. "Your eyes are about to fall out. Don't sweat it, man. If my daughter came home and told me she was pregnant with a White baby, I'd kick her ass."

Jimmy forced a smile.

"So," Arnold said. "Whatcha gonna do about it?"

"I dunno," Jimmy said. "I mean, my plate's kinda full with Clarice...." He almost said *dying*. "And it's not like I can force Pauline have an abortion. She's determined to keep it."

"Not in the way you're thinking, anyway."

Jimmy looked at Arnold. "What do you mean?" He'd heard about a guy who beat his daughter over at the Blue Fields projects a few years back, hoping the beating would induce a miscarriage. He didn't think Arnold was talking about anything like that though.

"Remember that shit we found at Old Nelly's?" Arnold asked.

Jimmy nodded.

"Well," Arnold said. "Some people believe that Old Nelly is a very powerful old lady. Maybe she can do something."

"You don't really believe in that garbage, do you?" Jimmy asked.

"You believe in God?" Arnold asked.

"Yeah," Jimmy said. He'd truly wondered the very same question lately but was ingrained to reply positively.

"So do I," Arnold said. "But probably not in the same way you do. There's too many religions for there to be a single God who created everything. But I do believe that *something* began it all and something more or less watches over us. It allows us to make our mistakes because even It can't change fate."

"That's no religion I've ever heard of," Jimmy said.

"It's just my beliefs," Arnold said. "Anyway, all religions touch It."

"How's this help me?" Jimmy asked.

"Do you really want your blonde-haired, blue-eyed girl to have a nigger-spic baby?" Arnold asked.

Jimmy jolted.

"Do you?" Arnold pushed.

"No," Jimmy said, unable to look at Arnold.

"Well, then," Arnold said. "I think Old Nelly can help stop it."

That night, Arnold accompanied Jimmy to Old Nelly's place. Jimmy felt guilty about leaving Clarice home alone (well, she was with Pauline, but might as well have been alone) but *something* had to be done.

Arnold knocked on the door and the small, hunched Black woman opened it, smiling a toothless grin and leaning on a cane.

"Ah," she said. "Come back but dis time 'tain't *my* pipes needin' fixin'." She cackled.

Arnold and Jimmy entered the apartment. The shades and curtains were drawn and hundreds of candles lit the room. Incense hung in the air.

"Sit down on de points," Old Nelly said.

Jimmy followed Old Nelly's arthritis-bent finger to a black mat that had been laid down. Painted in white was a triangle with strange symbols in it. Arnold sat on one angle and Jimmy sat on the angle to Arnold's right. Old Nelly slowly sat facing them. Near her, within easy reach, was a shoebox of stuff from her closet. He looked in and then looked up at Jimmy.

"Arnold heah tol' me yo' problem," Old Nelly said. Her brown eyes bore deep into Jimmy. "Don't like de mix, huh?"

Jimmy's face heated up.

Old Nelly cackled again. "Son, you know your toughts ain't right, and dat's good. Means de ol' dog can change. And if dat were de only problem, we wouldn't be sittin' here. But it's more dan dat. I'm helpin' your little girl more'n I'm helpin' you, believe you me!"

She pulled out a small baggy with gray powder in it. It looked like a baggy of cocaine, Jimmy had found enough of them in the empties to know what they looked like.

"Get it into your lil girl somehow," Old Nelly said.

"In a drink or something?" Jimmy asked.

"A drink, food, whatever," Old Nelly said. "Don't matter how. Just get it in her."

"Okay." Jimmy placed the powder in his shirt pocket.

"One last ting, dough," Old Nelly said. "It needs a pubic hair from a dyin' woman."

Out of the corner of Jimmy's eye he saw Arnold look down at the floor. Jimmy's mouth was dry and he nodded. It wasn't a problem.

"Hear me good now," Old Nelly said. "Usin' magic, *any* magic, costs you. Dis type of magic costs mo'. And dis shit here is some *nasty* magic. Once she drinks it, it's too late to turn back."

Jimmy nodded.

"And it *will* cost you, son," Old Nelly said. "Damn straight. Dis goan cost you."

They rode back to Jimmy's apartment house in silence. Arnold double-parked in front of the house and Jimmy waited for cars to pass before opening the door.

Just as Jimmy was about to step out, Arnold said, "You don't have to go through with this. There's nothing binding you. Not yet."

Jimmy thought about it. Clarice was sick and would soon be dead. He'd be left to handle everything, Pauline included. Pauline and her baby. Even if it didn't have African- and Mexican American blood, he couldn't handle his teenage daughter having a baby right now; not when she was incapable of taking care of herself.

"I know," he said.

Then Jimmy thanked Arnold, told him he'd see him at work tomorrow, and got out of the car.

Jimmy locked the door behind him. Rap music thumped from Pauline's bedroom but the rest of the apartment was silent. Clarice lay in bed, sleeping, her breath rattling. He didn't know how he'd go on once she died. Jimmy and Pauline hadn't gotten along since she was in middle school. Jimmy sighed and sat on the bed next to Clarice, remembering the first time they touched, the first time they kissed, the first time they made love. The way hair always seemed to fall over her right eye. The way her hugs felt. Hell, the way her coffee tasted. Thirty years of marriage rushed back to Jimmy and brought tears. He touched Clarice's face, ran a finger over the small swell of her right breast. Touched her flat, too-skinny belly, remembering the baby-fat that he'd kiss when they'd first started going together, the way he'd talk to it when she was carrying Pauline. His hand went beneath her pink cotton underwear that had faded and had worn thin, felt her bristling pubic hair between his fingers, and plucked one.

Clarice moaned and her eyes fluttered open. Jimmy's hand was with the other, in his lap, and he smiled down at her.

"I love you," she said.

"I love you, too," Jimmy said, leaned over, and kissed her forehead.

Clarice closed her eyes and went back to sleep.

Jimmy stood, holding the wiry pubic hair between the thumb and index finger of his left hand. He went to the kitchen and turned on the fire under the kettle. Once it whistled, he made two mugs of hot chocolate—the kind that comes with marshmallows—and mixed the powder and the broken up pubic hair into Pauline's Kermit the Frog mug. Then Jimmy took both mugs to Pauline's bedroom and knocked on the door. She opened it, saw her father, and her eyes fell to the mugs in his hands.

"Can we talk?" he asked.

It was the best conversation they'd had since she'd hit puberty. Jimmy began it by talking about Clarice's condition and then it went from there. He watched as Pauline drank the hot chocolate, drank it all, and felt his stomach tighten.

Pauline was scared. She hated what the cancer had done to Clarice and didn't want her to die. She'd been avoiding the whole thing, preferring to remember Clarice the way she'd been before the cancer began its handiwork—or at least before it had begun to show. She confessed she knew her relationship with Nigel Sanchez was a dead end but there was nothing she could do about the baby, although she was pro-choice, her choice was to keep the baby. The conversation ended with both of them weeping, hugging, and apologizing. When Jimmy left Pauline's room, his heart floated and he almost forgot about the potion he'd put in her hot chocolate. Almost.

The clock on the microwave told him it was 10:43 and he thought it felt later than that. He went to the bathroom, pissed, brushed his teeth, and went to his bedroom.

He noticed it the moment he entered the room. Silence. Jimmy had grown accustomed to Clarice's labored, congested breathing. Now it wasn't there. He sat on the edge of the bed and placed a hand on her forehead. It was cold.

Old Nelly had told him there'd be a price to pay.

Jimmy went back to Pauline's bedroom and told her. She wept. Jimmy held his daughter, told her it was all right, they knew it'd been coming. Then he told her he had to make some phone calls. He was on the wall phone in the kitchen when Pauline came out of her bedroom holding her stomach and went into the bathroom. A few moments later, she screamed.

The doctors decided that the shock of Clarice's death caused Pauline to miscarry. They were all surprised by the quick recovery she had, though. Jimmy was proud of the way Pauline handled herself the day of Clarice's funeral. She'd become a woman in the few days since Clarice's death and the miscarriage (for he'd been able to convince himself that's what had really happened, not some black magic bullshit).

That night, Jimmy went to bed, felt the empty spot where Clarice had lay for thirty years, and felt a mix of grief and pride. God, he missed her. God, he was so proud of the daughter she'd helped raise. He went to sleep thinking maybe he wasn't as unlucky as he'd always thought.

He dreamed she was with him, lying in bed and telling him her hopes and dreams. They kissed and made love. It was a great dream. When the alarm clock woke him up he almost felt her behind him. He turned around, intending to add the image of her in his mind's eye to the empty spot that remained.

Jimmy went cold and his heart jolted. Clarice lay looking at him, smiling, eyes wide. Dirt and grass clung to her hair and soil smudged her face.

"Dey's always a price to pay," she rasped. The voice wasn't Clarice's, though, but the scratchy one that had belonged to Old Nelly Janks. Then she cackled.

Jimmy somehow managed to hold back a scream. He continued to hold it back every morning thereafter, too.

SOMETHING IN THE PIPES

Stuart Kress had a tickle in his chest. Again. First the tickle and within moments, breathing became a chore. It seemed that each time he inhaled, the tickle grew worse. The thought came before he could stop it:

Please don't let me die. Not now. Not here.

Stuart looked around the subway car at the other passengers packed inside. His heart pounded and ears rang. It felt as though a thick towel had been balled up and shoved so far down his throat that its little tag tickled the inside of his chest.

I told you to go to the doctor, Melanie said. *I've told you and told you but do you listen?*

The subway car tilted. No, it *felt* like the subway car tilted but it only shook. Stuart closed his eyes against the oncoming dizziness and grasped tighter to the rail.

The tickle stopped and he breathed easily again. The dizziness lifted and the subway car returned to normal. A headache lingered behind his eyes along with the fear that the tickle was getting worse and would kill him.

Stuart visited the doctor the next day. Not long into the visit he decided he didn't like Dr. Wagner very much. First, the doctor called him Stu—which Stuart loathed (Stu wasn't a name, it was a food, like soup but not really)—and then the doctor told Stuart he had to go to the hospital for tests.

That meant two days of no work. His supervisor wouldn't be pleased. One less computer programmer at a cubicle in a room of twenty cubicles and eighteen programmers (one of the cubicles housed a secretary, the other dead computers) would set work back .9893874 seconds. Stuart didn't kid himself; he was dispensable.

After the appointment he went to work, told his supervisor about the extra day he needed, and worked until 4:35, when he wrapped things up. At five he was out the office door and by 6:30, walking through his apartment door.

"What happened at the doctor's?" Melanie asked before the door had closed.

"I have to go to the hospital for some tests," Stuart said. "They'll probably find lung cancer and give me six months to live."

"Hm," she said and then inquired about what side he'd like with that night's dinner.

The goddamn hospital was a maze and Stuart was five minutes late for his appointment. Now, sitting and waiting, he almost wished he hadn't quit smoking two years ago. To hell with the lung cancer (he'd convinced himself in the twenty-four hours that that's what the tickle was), he'd rather have the nicotine's calming effect.

After half an hour of waiting, a woman wearing light blue scrubs approached him.

"Mr. Kress?" she said, handing him johnnies. "Could you put these on, this one faces the front, this one goes over like a robe. The changing stations are right there. When you're done, we can begin the X-rays."

Once in the johnnies, feeling like Asshole #1, Stuart followed the nurse to the X-ray room where he met a woman doctor. One look at the X-ray table and machine caused his scrotum to tighten and his hairs to stand.

By the time the tests ended and they released him (he wondered how come the only places that released people were hospitals and prisons?) the day was lost. Stuart went home and watched reruns until Melanie came home.

"What did they say?" she asked.

"They ran some tests, listened to my lungs, and that was about it. They said someone would call me if they found something."

On both days that he'd missed work, he'd had trouble breathing and had felt the tickle. The morning after the tests, Stuart awoke with the tickle. He felt as though he'd been exercising and was out of breath.

On the subway ride to work, Stuart saw an old man with an oxygen tank, a clear plastic tube going around his face and up his nose. The man had to have been in his seventies. Had Stuart been seventy—shit, if he'd been over fifty—he wouldn't mind having health problems so much, but he was only in his thirties, too young to be sick.

At the office, the tickle and the heavy breathing annoyed the shit out of him but he did his work. His supervisor asked how he felt and Stuart said fine. The supervisor didn't give a flying monkey's cock how Stuart felt, he just wanted to know if Stuart were dying so he could start looking for someone else because we all know how long *that* can take.

Stuart's phone rang a little after nine and he placed his headset on.

"Stu Kress?" It was Dr. Wagner.

"This is *Stuart* Kress, yes."

"Mr. Kress," the doctor said. "I think we need to talk."

At four o'clock that afternoon, with the tickle still persistent, Stuart sat in a bar, drunk. They'd found something. A large mass, Dr. Wagner had said. They wanted to run more tests ASAP. Stuart didn't remember the rest.

Leaving the doctor's office and getting to the bar was a blur that didn't really matter. Nothing mattered now. He was dying. That's what it all came down to. That's what everything came down to. From the moment we're born, we're dying. Stuart sat at the bar speaking of such philosophies for a while. Finally, the bartender, a small man with a bulbous nose—more from boxing than from drinking, Stuart guessed—came over and asked him to shut his mouth about death and that happy crappy.

"You're scaring away my customers," the bartender said.

Stuart responded by saluting with his glass of scotch and continued drinking.

The tickle had grown worse. Instead of remaining in Stuart's chest, it'd moved up into his throat. He coughed a few times, feeling nauseated. Stuart stumbled off the stool and made his way to the men's room. He went to a stall, splashing through someone's piss, and bent his knees. Here it came.

He hacked once, twice, three times but nothing came up. The tickle felt closer to the top of his throat. Even the alcohol hadn't dissuaded it.

Stuart left the bathroom and found the bartender waiting outside the door.

"I think it's time to call it a day, fella," the bartender.

"The name is Stuart, *fella.*"

"I don't care if the name's Jesus Christ and you're here waiting for Elvis and Marilyn Monroe to come in, it's time to call it a day, *Stu.*"

"The name's Stuart." A big guy with bulging muscles and tattoos strutted over. "Stu is a food, like soouu—"

He passed out.

He had to puke. Stuart opened his eyes. Melanie looked down at him, disgusted.

"Do you know how awful it is to have to leave work early to pick up your drunken husband?" she asked.

Stuart retched and she stepped back.

"Not on the carpet! Get in the bathroom!"

Stuart got up, fell, and got up again. He made his way to the bathroom, knelt at the Altar of the Toilet, and waited. And waited. After nearly ten minutes, Melanie came in.

"Are you okay?" she asked.

"I'm dying," he said and got up. The tickle in his throat and a new pressure in his chest convinced him of this.

"Serves you right. Drinking in the afternoon...."

"No, no, no. I mean I'm really dying."

Realization flashed in her eyes. "You mean...the doctor...?"

"Well," Stuart said and slid past her, into the hallway. "He didn't say I was dying but they found something in the X-rays so I'm sure I'm close."

Melanie, for the first time since they'd met, was speechless.

She followed him down the hall to the living room.

"I think it's too late," Stuart said. "The tickle is growing."

"Growing?"

"Yeah. It's in my throat now. And where it was before there's...I don't know, some sort of pressure."

"Is there anything I can do?" Melanie asked.

Before he could answer, the pressure became pain and Stuart gasped.

"Are you okay?" Melanie asked.

"I..." A hitch of pain. "...don't know."

It felt like he had to vomit. His strength dissipated and he fell to his knees.

"Oh my God," Melanie said, looking around. "What can I do? Call 911."

She grabbed the phone on the coffee table and dialed. Meanwhile, Stuart knelt on the floor, retching. The tickle moved up the back of his throat and touched the uvula, jiggling it. Stuart gagged and the tickle—tickles—moved. Something poked at the roof of his mouth. He bit down on a hard, hairy thing and pain exploded in his upper chest, just below the neck, as if something had bitten him on the inside. Stuart retched again and saw a tubular black...*thing* coming out of his mouth, small hairs bristling.

Melanie had been talking to the operator and stopped. She looked at Stuart, eyes wide.

The more he retched, the longer the hairy black thing grew. Then came another, the hairs tickling his tongue and the roof of his mouth. Stuart couldn't breath and the world swam.

The two hairy black things bent and pushed against his face. Two more of them came out of his mouth and pushed until a furry black...*thing* with pincers exited his mouth, a string of drool connecting its underbelly to Stuart's bottom lip. Stuart sucked in a large breath and choked. The insectile thing scuttled across the living room and turned into the hallway. Stuart rolled to his side and vomited.

Melanie stood frozen, staring down the hall. Stuart forced himself to his feet, grabbed a broom from a closet, and went to the bedroom at the end of the hall. Nothing. Then he went into the bathroom. He turned on the light in time to see the thing disappearing down the toilet drain.

Melanie came in behind him, sniffling and wiping at her eyes but already regaining control of herself.

The tickle was gone. That's all it had been. Stuart was a little relieved despite the hows and whys.

"Honey?" Melanie said. She reserved that particular term of endearment for when she was going to get on his case.

"Yes, sweetheart?" Stuart asked, realizing their marriage was probably over.

"What if it left eggs?"

Stuart stared at the toilet, unable to respond. He told himself, though, that his stomach pains were a result of the vomiting and stress. And nothing else.

FUN GUS THE TAP DANCE MAN

Ryan noticed the suitcase sitting on the tiled floor the moment he arrived. Luggage lying around the bus station's ticket booth wasn't an oddity but something about this suitcase not only made Ryan notice it, but also made him fixate on it. Mostly he saw those pieces of nylon, water-resistant luggage so prevalent in today's commuter world. This suitcase was leather and solid, shell-like. It was dark brown with tan leather around the edges. The handle had the same tan leather. Plain metal clasps with small locks kept it closed.

The suitcase brought forth images of actors long dead, wearing suits with round straw hats that one sometimes saw nowadays made from Styrofoam at political rallies. He could see a man rushing toward a train that was about to leave, his overcoat draped over an arm and the suitcase clutched with white knuckles. Gene Kelly or Frank Sinatra or maybe even Bing Crosby could play the man.

Fun Gus the Tap Dance Man, a voice said and Ryan smiled. His imagination was too vivid sometimes.

He went through his Saturday morning ritual of opening the Harden Bus Station. He changed the security videos, started up the ticket computer, counted the drawer, and unlocked the doors only five minutes past six, the time he should have opened. No one waited outside this morning. Back in the ticket booth, Ryan unzipped his backpack, ready to pull out the drawings he'd brought with him, when his eyes again fell on the suitcase.

He abandoned his backpack and easily lifted the almost empty suitcase onto a wheeled chair. The scuffed suitcase's bottom corner was a little caved in. The suitcase wasn't large but could hold a change or two of clothes.

Two tags were tied to the handle with strings. One was a plain tag that a person could buy just about anywhere. The name on it was Gustav. The second tag had the Greyhound logo at the top and resembled one of the tickets issued in New York. The tag had been through a lot. The printing on it was faded and watermarks had smudged some of the ink, making it nearly illegible. A few of the destinations that could still be made out were: Centerville, MS; Kent, OH; New York, NY; Laramie, WY; and the last destination was Harden, MA. Ryan stared at this tag and something about it made his skin prickle. He'd never seen anything like this before. Odder still were the numbers near the destinations: 1943, 1970, 1984, 1998. Harden's number was 2007.

A customer came to the window and Ryan put the suitcase back. After he'd sold a ticket (one way, Boston), he looked at the suitcase and thought about opening it.

He worked a six-hour shift on Saturdays. The pay was good, he was able to work at his art or study, but that Saturday, with each passing hour, he focused on the suitcase. His wife, Rachel, would've laughed at him. Even Meghan, his five-year-old, wouldn't be afraid of the damn thing.

Ryan left the station at two. He didn't say anything about the suitcase to George, the older man who covered two to closing. George didn't seem to notice it. Whatever fixation Ryan felt toward the suitcase had lessened by the time he was half a mile away from the bus station and the suitcase soon retreated to the back of his mind.

If Ryan drank, he'd drown everything out. He didn't smoke, either, and didn't do drugs. Instead, he munched on Doritos as Rachel and Meghan lay in bed in the other room, watching TV.

Why did he and Rachel have to fight so goddamn much lately? What did she want with him? He was doing the best he could. She'd *known* when they'd met almost ten years ago that he was an artist. Sooner or later he'd be able to support them with it. He knew it and she used to know it, too. So why did she bust his balls about it? He'd gone back to college for them, for chrissakes. What else did she want?

The envelopes still lay strewn on the floor. The bills within, small pieces of paper, loomed as tall as any mountain. His mission was to climb that mountain and conquer it. But how? How when the economy sucked, when his job sucked, when his life sucked?

It was his fault, of course. Had he originally stayed in college, had he gotten a degree, he could've held a real job. Had he not stayed home and raised their daughter they wouldn't have this problem.

Disgusted with self-pity and -loathing, he closed the bag of chips and picked up the bills. Cable, phone, gas, electric, and credit cards that couldn't be used anymore. He sighed. The only other mail that had come in today was a rejection from *Dim Findings*, a horror fiction magazine, where he'd sent what he'd believed was a fairly disturbing drawing. It wasn't right for them, though, so it had come back with a form rejection. The Doritos went back in the small kitchen and Ryan went to the computer to look up some markets for his art. Instead, he was distracted. Soon, two hours had passed, the television in his bedroom had gone off (programmed to do so, no doubt; his wife and daughter always fell asleep before they could turn it off), and it was too late to do anything productive. Again, disgusted with himself, he threw out a few used tissues, turned off the computer, and went to bed in his daughter's empty bed.

Through the mists of sleep, someone shook him. When Ryan opened his eyes, it wasn't his daughter's bedroom he was in but a large room with several hundred bunks. A pale man with close-cropped hair and wearing older-style military fatigues stood over him.

"It's time," the man said, his accent turned it to *tahm*. "We're goan get them niggers."

"What?" Ryan asked, sitting up. The brown leather suitcase from the bus station lay on a footlocker at the foot of his bunk. It looked brand new. An up-tempo piano tune seemed to come from it but was muted by the sounds of other soldiers getting ready.

Ryan realized vaguely that this was a dream. But why

the hell dream himself into the military with someone with a southern accent using the N-word? Time and space shifted and he found himself dressed in fatigues and standing outside. There were several hundred men, all white, standing around him. Someone pressed a rifle into his hands. In the distance, the up-tempo piano music continued.

"Your orders are simple," said a commanding officer. "Go into the niggers' barracks and get them out here." *Heah*. "No uppity Yankee niggers are goanna try to run *this* place."

The realization of what was happening bloomed in Ryan's head and he found himself mentally backing up, trying to change the dream just as he always tried to do when dreams became nightmares. The officer looked at him.

"What you doin'?" he asked.

"This is fucked-up," Ryan said trying to change the dream or at least wake up.

The officer glared at him. He took several steps toward Ryan, removing a pistol from his holster, and put the barrel against Ryan's forehead. He smelled the pistol's oil.

"Insubordination during wartime is punishable by death," the officer said, his Southern accent seeming to relish the words. "Are you goanna follow orders or are you goanna join the niggers?"

Ryan screamed at himself to wake up. He didn't, though. His eyes held the officer's cold, crazed blue eyes, and the dream shifted. Things blurred, coming and going. In the end, Ryan stood outside again. Now, though, he and the other white soldiers stood in front of different barracks with hundreds, maybe thousands, of Black men in front of them. The Black men, many crying, mostly still in their underwear, remained still.

"We're gonna show these uppity Yankee niggers how things're done in Miss'ippi," another officer announced farther away from Ryan. "We can't trust 'em, can we? I know some of you white Yanks don't agree, but the other Southern Gentlemen here at Camp Van Dorn know what I'm sayin' is the *truth*. They'll kill you on the battlefield, gentlemen. Dogs are good but can bite anytime. Niggers are even more dangerous. They'd just as soon kill one-a y'all than kill one-a Hitler's men or a yella gook."

The Black men were beginning to realize that the harassment was over. The beatings, the rude comments, the oppression was done. Several broke from the group and ran to the tall fences. They began climbing trees to get over.

Ryan blinked. Down the line between the white and Black was a man. He wore white slacks and shoes, and a red and white striped jacket over a white shirt with a black bowtie. He tap danced slowly on the grass, defying logic and physics, and held his round-brimmed straw hat over his head. The suitcase was now open at his feet with a few quarters inside. He danced to the faint, never-ending piano music.

"Ready," the second officer called.

Rifles went up.

Ryan's heart rammed against his chest. *Wake up!* he told himself.

"Aim!" the second officer yelled.

The first officer came up behind Ryan, the steel barrel of his gun against the back of Ryan's neck. Shaking, his arms raised the rifle on their own.

He couldn't do it. He'd die before killing another human. But—

"*FIRE!*" the officers called.

Rifle fire crackled along the line of white soldiers. Black heads opened, Black chests opened, Black arms were taken off. Black men fell from trees where they'd tried to hide, screaming. More gunfire. Blood, bone, brains, and other organs splashed the grass and the sound of hundreds and hundreds of people dropping into the mess filled the night sky. The screams and cries were almost deafening, louder even than the multiple rifle shots.

One Black man stood staring at Ryan, defiant.

"Victory at Home," the Black man said.

"You have one last chance," the officer whispered into Ryan's ear.

"Victory Abroad," the Black man said.

Meghan... Ryan thought as he squeezed the trigger and—

He sat up, breath coming in gasps, heart ramming. Somehow as the night progressed, he found a way to push back the image of the Black man's face opening up and spraying skull and brains. The image of the suitcase lying on the footlocker as well as at the tap-dancing man's feet would not go away, though.

Sunday and Monday passed without much happening. Tuesday was a tough day. Ryan had to get up early to take Rachel to work, then he brought Meghan to school, and then he went to school. He had two classes there, left at a quarter to two, and rushed to get Meghan. By three he was exhausted and still had reading, studying, and a paper to write. At suppertime he'd have to pick Rachel up from work. Meghan asked him to play but he just didn't have enough energy. She went in her bedroom and began playing with her toy horses. Ryan sat back, turned on CNN to briefly see what kind of mess they were all in before he began his schoolwork. His eyes soon slipped shut.

The piano music chilled him. There were more soldiers, too. Though this time he wasn't among them. This time, he was among a different army. This army comprised of young adults, most of them barely in their twenties. Long hair, peace signs, banners and picket signs waved. The other army walked away from the young men and women.

"No war in Vietnam!" a girl standing near him chanted at the top of her lungs.

She had long, straight hair, and clutched a notebook that had KENT STATE printed on the cover. Ryan's mouth went dry as he realized where he was. The protestors' sounds faded but the piano played its tune. The tap-dancing man danced amidst the students in slow motion, out of sync with the world around him.

The retreating soldiers turned and open fired for no apparent reason. The girl next to Ryan was thrown back as a bullet tore through her chest. She landed with a thud, dead. The piano music continued. The girl turned her head and looked at Ryan with her dead eyes.

"Daddy," she said in Meghan's voice and—

Ryan jolted awake with a shout. Meghan screamed and jumped

back, surprised. A moment later she cried. Ryan hugged her.

"It's okay," he whispered. "Everything's fine. I'm sorry I scared you."

"You were talking in your sleep," Meghan said against his chest. "You scared me."

"I'm sorry," he repeated. He hoped Meghan didn't feel his trembling.

He called the bus station. His manager, Liz, answered.

"Hi, Liz. It's Ryan. I know this is going to sound crazy, but is that suitcase still there?"

"Which one?"

"An older one. Brown leather. Kinda beaten up."

"That one. Yeah, it's here. Why? Do you know who it belongs to?"

Fun Gus the Tap Dance Man, Ryan thought. "No," he said. "I was just wondering if it was still there."

A bill collector called Thursday afternoon and gave him a hard time, cutting Ryan off at just about every sentence. The bill collector threatened to sue, which was something he couldn't threaten because of federal consumer law. Still, the phone call left Ryan shaken.

That night he and Rachel argued again. This time it was over sex. They hadn't had sex in almost a month, with two months having passed between that time and a similar amount the time before. Since Meghan had been born five years before, he and Rachel's sex life had just about dried up.

"I just worked all day," she said. "If you worked all day you wouldn't feel like it either."

"What do you mean? I had school today and then I was with Meghan. Staying with her isn't the easiest task in the world. I'm tired, too."

"Well, I don't feel like it."

"I'm sick of this shit," Ryan said. "For chrissakes, why did you marry me? Why be married if we're going to live like fucking roommates?"

"Don't swear at me," Rachel said.

"Why the fuck not? Everything's crumbling down around me and I can't let it out?"

"How is that my fault?"

"I never wanted this," Ryan yelled. "*You* stopped taking the pill and never told me. *You* wanted this. *I* never wanted any of this!"

Rachel stared at him. Tears shimmered in her eyes. Ryan felt his face flush and heard his words echo through his head. He opened his mouth, ready to speak, when Meghan's voice interrupted him.

"You didn't want me, Daddy?"

The question sliced into his heart. He looked at her. She shimmered as tears filled his eyes.

"I..." he said but didn't know how to finish. Finally, he settled on, "I love you."

"I love you, too, Daddy," Meghan said. She sounded sad when she spoke.

The vaudevillian piano music played somewhere in the humid streets of New York. Ryan walked behind a little Puerto Rican girl with a 1984 Summer Olympics tee shirt on. She stood out from her soft, drab surroundings, seeming to radiate with light and color. She turned into an alley, no doubt a short cut. His perspective shifted and he soon stood a few feet from where he'd been a moment before. A tall white man with red cheeks, crazed black hair, and thick, round eyeglasses entered the alley, licking his lips. In his hands was the brown leather suitcase.

Ryan's heart rammed. He wanted to wake up but couldn't. Without moving his feet, he followed the man into the alley. He and the girl were gone. An overflowing dumpster was against the right hand wall and trash was strewn about. Behind the dumpster was an alcove with a door set back several feet. Grunting came from behind the wall. The girl's voice.

Turn around, his mind screamed and he turned, but the dream shifted and instead of turning away from the alley, Ryan now stood on the other side of the dumpster. At the mouth of the alley, where he'd just stood, was the tap dance man. Ryan looked away from the dancing man to the alcove. The suitcase lay open on the ground filled with photographs. A camera's flash popped. When the white faded, Ryan saw the little girl lying naked near the steel door, her chest open and a beer bottle jutting from her—

His eyes snapped open and he held the rising bile back enough to get to the bathroom. After puking he sat against the toilet and sobbed. What the fuck was happening? *Why* was it happening? He didn't believe in the supernatural, so how come this suitcase—and he *knew* it was the suitcase—brought these...visions?

You're under a lot of stress, he told himself. *Your artwork's not selling. You're bogged down in schoolwork. The family life is going to hell.*

Being rational wasn't working. Maybe he should visit the counselor at the school's crisis center.

Ryan stood on quivering legs and went into his bedroom where Rachel and Meghan slept. Meghan snored softly. Rachel's inhaled and exhaled slowly. They had no clue he stood over them, watching. He bent and kissed Meghan's cheek, her flesh warm and soft under his lips. She didn't even stir. He could've taken a hammer and smashed her head open and she wouldn't know until it was too late.

The weight of the thought struck him. It had floated up from the dregs of his mind. He went cold and the hair over his body bristled. He went to the living room—was he floating?—and fell onto the couch. What was happening to him?

He didn't go back to sleep that night. He still sat on the couch, nervous, eyes aching, when Friday dawned and the dull light entered the living room. Soon, he heard the bed creak as Rachel rose. He tracked the sounds of her movement: feet shuffling to the bathroom, the lid hitting the tank, the tinkling of her piss. The toilet flushed and she came into the living room, stopping when she saw him.

"Are you okay?" she asked, genuine concern in her voice. It only touched his heart a little, though, and he barely noticed the inner voice pointing out that she loved him, something he knew and saw in her eyes whenever they spoke of the future.

"Had a nightmare," he said. "A bad one."

"Oh." She didn't know what else to say so went into the kitchen to start the coffee. She didn't offer to make him tea. He didn't ask.

He didn't bother going to school. Instead, he brought Rachel to work, Meghan to school, and returned home. He went online.

He knew about the tragedy in Kent State in 1970, of course, but looked up the key words *Van Dorn* and *Centerville, Mississippi*. Sure enough, he found out about a controversy. Over a thousand Black soldiers were allegedly shot dead during World War II, their bodies transferred by train to another part of Camp Van Dorn and buried. The alleged incident was disputed for lack of hard evidence, but Ryan had been there. The suitcase had brought him there in his sleep. He'd never heard of it beforehand.

In 1984 there had been a rash of child killings in New York, all girls, all between ten and thirteen. There was little news of this, though, only a website dedicated to a little girl named Yolanda Cruz. He recognized her face. No killer had ever been found. Ryan had been seven that summer, living in Harden. He wouldn't have known Yolanda Cruz. Not at all.

He wanted to try and find out what was happening to him but where would he go? What website could possibly answer his questions? Ryan had gone online in the hopes of making himself feel better. Instead, he felt worse. The room around him felt far removed, a painting surrounding him instead of an actual, three-dimensional environment.

There had to be something he could do. Maybe if he got rid of the suitcase, it would stop. But how? Just go into the bus station, take it, and burn it? Take it to the Fairview Bridge and drop it into the river?

That idea seemed appealing. Maybe set it on fire *and* drop it. Ryan smiled.

That night he walked through Wyoming as two men beat and tied a nude young man to a fence, calling him a fucking fag and telling him God didn't love faggots and Ryan carried the suitcase away, which had become heavy as the road became a street filled with Nazi soldiers and he clutched the suitcase tight as they loaded him onto the back of a truck and though he didn't understand German or Polish, knew what was happening, where the truck would go, but everything shifted and he carried the suitcase away from the room it had been in, its owner no doubt screaming in one of the massive ovens that took up so much space in Dachau, but the death camp became a Chinese public square and a college student was crushed under a tank and Ryan closed his eyes, the piano music becoming louder, and when he opened his eyes the suitcase lay open on a bed in a small apartment as Jeffrey Dahmer placed a head in a plastic bag, the refrigerator door open behind him and images, smells, and sounds engulfed him, and the tap dancing man danced throughout, entertaining no one, the piano music swelling until it took over his mind and one chord repeated louder than the others, over and over, repeated and became a word, became *kill, kill*

kill
KILL—

Ryan awoke at four. He needed no more sleep. He went to the bathroom, and showered. He watched Rachel and Meghan as he dressed. He could do anything to them right now without their knowing.

He closed his eyes against the thought, against the voice telling him it was okay, it was all right. He grabbed his keys and jacket and left the apartment.

The suitcase hadn't moved in seven days. It was right where he'd left it. Why should anyone have moved it? It didn't talk to *them*. He lifted the suitcase and it still felt empty though something moved inside. He placed it on the counter. Whatever was inside wasn't very substantial.

Ryan took a deep breath. The clasps snapped up. He lifted the suitcase's lid.

His feet went cold and his flesh tingled. He swallowed his heart back down and removed the photograph of Fun Gus the Tap Dance Man with a trembling hand. The old photograph had yellowed and browned around the edges. Some of the solution on top had begun cracking and peeling. Still, even though water (and other…stuff) had stained the picture, Fun Gus's face was clearly visible. Ryan recognized him. He realized, up until that point, in the dreams, Fun Gus's face had never quite registered with him. Now it did. He recognized the eyes and the smile, though Fun Gus's features were much more demented than what Ryan usually saw in the mirror.

Take it to the bridge, he told himself. *Get rid of this evil thing.*

But the suitcase held so much power, power that rushed through him in waves. If he got rid of this suitcase someone else would find it. They'd take it and….

With a gulp, Ryan closed the suitcase. Clutching it, he left the bus station.

In the vacant lot next to his apartment house, Ryan watched the old photograph burn until only ashes remained. Then he took the suitcase inside.

It was only six-thirty. The apartment was silent. Ryan didn't make a sound as he entered the bedroom. He looked down at his sleeping wife and daughter. Images of the butcher knife on the counter, the hammer in the toolbox, the—

He closed his eyes against the impulses flowing from the suitcase, up his arm, into his mind. It seemed each *flub-dub, flub-dub* of his heart changed to *slaugh-ter, slaugh-ter.* Trembling, he laid the suitcase on the floor, opened it, caught a flash of knives and chains before they disappeared, and went to the task of packing. Several pair of underwear and socks. Jeans and some shirts. He closed the suitcase with a click and stood.

Ryan looked one last time at his wife and daughter, heart ramming, body shaking. The impulse was so goddamn strong. He leaned over Rachel and kissed her forehead, then kissed Meghan. He loved them—God, he loved them—but this was for the best.

He left. The impulses still radiated from the suitcase but Ryan ignored them. It was time to break the chain. It was time to break the hate. It was time to break.

MOMMY'S BABY DON'T NEED TO GROW UP

When I was ten years old, my mother got pregnant and I found myself praying that she'd miscarry. She talked about getting an abortion but didn't. She told me one night after a few too many drinks that this was her chance to raise a good daughter, not a fuck-up like me.

My sister, Kristen, was born April 27, 1984, two months before my eleventh birthday. I had already been discarded, though; allowed to take care of myself.

I remember one night about two months after her birth, standing over Kristen's crib. I held a tissue to my nose but still felt blood roll down my upper lip and around my mouth. My Mom had beaten me that night because I hadn't taken the trash out. I'd been home alone with a two-month-old and afraid to go outside with the trash—we didn't live in the best neighborhood in the city.

I stared at Kristen for a long time. She lay still, eyes closed, her tiny breaths the only proof that she was alive. I didn't want her to go through what I'd gone—and was still going—through. Sure, Mom called her "Mommy's Baby" and promised nothing would ever happen to her, but I knew Mom wasn't capable of keeping promises. *Any* promises. I thought about taking my pillow from the nearby bed and smothering her. Or maybe the revolver in Mom's underwear drawer.

Then Kristen began snoring these tiny snores that captured my heart and I couldn't go through with it.

I regretted not doing it many times afterward.

I regretted it the day, almost two years later, when I started my period and Mom forced me to go to school with the biggest goddamn pad you've ever seen. I was made fun of the whole day. I'd been a target ever since third grade when the other kids started getting the idea that some people were shabby and others were chic. I was one of the shabby. That day, though, with the pad, they were ruthless.

"Look at Cheryl," they'd call. "She's wearing a diaper."

Even the other kids who were always being fucked with jumped on me that day. Maybe they were hoping to get status. Maybe they were so glad it wasn't them they'd forgotten what it felt like to get your soul torn apart. Maybe they were just assholes. Whatever, that day I was crushed.

I went home crying. I entered the house trying to hide my tears. Mom wasn't one who cared much for them, thinking they were a sign of weakness. She held a napping Kristen while watching her soaps and, like an eagle zeroing in on a field mouse, saw my tear-slicked cheeks.

"Why are you crying?" she said, her voice hard.

I didn't want to tell her but I couldn't stop myself. Verbal diarrhea flowed. The size of my pad, the other kids' taunting, everything. I stared at the worn tan carpet the entire time. When I was done I looked up. I'd hoped to see a face filled with understanding, the face of a woman who was willing to comfort her thirteen-year-old daughter. Instead, I saw a face filled with rage. Her eyes glared and her mouth was set, the lines around it looking chiseled.

"Come here," she said through clenched teeth.

My mother carefully placed Kristen on the couch next to her as I approached. Once Kristen was down, my mother swung around and punched me in the stomach. The cramps had been bad all day and this was like dying. I fell to the floor, unable to breathe, unable to move.

"You little bitch," she said over me. "I'm not rich. I can't afford gourmet fuckin' tampons or those skinny pads. You want 'em? Get off your fat ass and get a job."

"You hurt me," I gasped and stood, clutching my belly.

"Life hurts," Mom said. "Deal with it."

Then she sat again and looked at the sleeping Kristen. "I hope Mommy's Baby don't grow up to be like *her*," she said. "As a matter of fact, I hope Mommy's Baby don't grow up at all."

I was leaving the room by that point but I heard something in my mother's voice I recognized immediately although I'd never heard it spoken toward me: love.

Christmas Day, 1988, she broke Kristen's arm. My mother had made Christmas cookies for her. I was fifteen. I had smelled the baking cookies in the morning. I listened to the Madonna CD I got for my present and watched Kristen look at the set of picture books she'd received, then play with her new baby doll. Kristen was four but very smart for her age. She knew that things weren't right in our home.

"They're done," my mother called from the kitchen and Kristen stood.

"C'mon, Cheryl," she said. "Let's get the cookies."

Captured by the magical joy in her voice, I went to the kitchen with her.

Mom stood next to the small kitchen table with a paper plate of cookies on it. They were sugar cookies shaped like Christmas trees, snowmen, and snowflakes with red and green sugar sprinkled on them. Mom smiled at Kristen but the smile melted when she saw me.

"These are Kristen's cookies," she said, looking me over. "I don't think you need no more sweets."

I nodded, turned around, and went to the bedroom Kristen and I shared. I lay on my bed and hid my face in the pillow. I didn't cry. I was used to being treated like shit and fantasized about escaping. In the small pocket of air I'd allowed myself, the cookie smell grew stronger and I looked up. Kristen stood with two cookies held out to me.

"Don't tell Mommy," she whispered.

I stared at her. To my knowledge, this was the first time Mommy's Baby disobeyed her. I couldn't help smiling as I took the cookies, Kristen's smile was infectious.

"I said she couldn't have none, you little shit!" Mom screamed.

Kristen turned and Mom grabbed her arm. "Come on," she said. "You're gettin' a spankin'."

"But—" Kristen cried, trying to pull herself away.

"Here!" I shouted. "Take the goddamn cookies!"

Mom stopped and stared at me in disbelief. How could I have the audacity? Then she screamed, *"DON'T YOU SWEAR AT ME, YOU LITTLE BITCH!"*

She yanked Kristen out of the way, ready to attack me, but stopped when a pop-crack filled the room. A moment of silence followed until Kristen's wails shattered it.

After they'd returned from the hospital that night, Kristen's arm in a cast, I received the worst beating of my life. I went to bed bruised and bloodied and looked at Kristen sleeping, breathing unevenly, her small cast seeming to glow in the night.

If I'd only done it, I thought. *She would never have to deal with this shit.* Those thoughts repeated themselves until I finally fell asleep.

Mom had been on the edge of sanity for as long as I can remember. I think she fell off when she broke Kristen's arm. Almost every day after that she'd tell Kristen or herself how she wished Mommy's Baby didn't need to grow up. She'd wake up after a night of heavy drinking (which was almost every day) and using drugs (which was more sporadic...at first), find she'd beaten both of us, and hold Kristen, crying about how she wished Mommy's Baby didn't need to grow up.

I was sixteen, almost seventeen, and Kristen was seven when it happened. I missed my period. No cramps, no blood, nothing. And, of course, Mom noticed. Mom wouldn't have noticed if I'd walked into our small apartment with my neck slit open—unless I was bleeding on the carpet, then she might notice and beat me—but she noticed my late period, which had come and gone on time as surely as the hours of the day since I was thirteen.

Exactly one week after the day my period should've started, Mom told me to get dressed but to stay in my room while she brought Kristen to the school bus. She took me to the clinic and they ran a test. I was pregnant. Mom thanked the doctor, the picture of calmness, and brought me home. At the clinic and on the way home, she acted calm but I felt the rage simmering below the surface. Once we got home, she beat me. At one point I blacked out as she punched me in the stomach over and over.

When I came to, the house was silent. I stood on rubbery legs and walked through the apartment. Mom was gone. It was only one o'clock in the afternoon and I couldn't think of where she could've gone. I was too tired and in too much pain to care. I briefly considered grabbing my few prized possessions and running away. Instead, I went to bed. I couldn't leave Kristen.

When I awoke again, the digital alarm clock on the night-stand told me it was five after two. Mom stood in the doorway.

"How do you feel?" she asked. She wasn't concerned, just curious.

I opened my mouth to answer but stopped. How did I feel? I wasn't sure. I felt...strange. I tried sitting up but couldn't move. I found I was tied to the bed with rope going over the edge of the mattress, most likely tied to the bed frame. My legs were also tied, the rope digging into my ankles. I was naked from the waist down and lay in a puddle of gore. A bloody, unwound clothes hanger lay on the bed like some hideous snake whose bloody head reached my knees while its tail slithered between my ankles.

"No," I whispered as reality began to swim away.

"I took care of your problem, slut," Mom said.

"No," I cried.

"From now on, keep your fishhole closed," she said.

"NO!" I screamed.

In an instant she was over me and she pounded me once, twice in the face. I sank into an ocean of gray but still noticed, on a chair between Kristen's bed and mine, an electric knife and a box of matches. Then the gray became black.

Kristen's screaming woke me up. I looked over and saw Mom struggling to tie Kristen to her bed with the ropes that had held me. Kristen was small and skinny and seemed to be able to con-tort herself any way she wanted.

"Keep still," Mom grunted. She'd managed to tie one of Kristen's hands.

"NOOOooo!" screamed Kristen.

"I *have* to," Mom told her, crying. "It's for your own good."

"Pleeeeasse, Mommy." Kristen sobbed. "I'll be good."

Kristen's other hand was tied.

"Mom," I said. "What're you doing?"

She looked at me with eyes filled with nothing but disgust. "I don't want her to grow up," she said. "I made mistakes with you, I can't make them again."

"Mommy!" Kristen kicked out and she connected hard with my mother's stomach.

Mom jumped on top of Kristen and pounded her face until Kristen lay still. I tried to move, tried to stop her, but the pain was too much and I was too weak, perhaps even drugged. Mom stood and took two belts from old outfits. I went cold as she fastened first one, then the other to each of Kristen's naked legs, a few inches above the knees. The she lifted the electric knife from the chair and plugged it into the socket between our beds.

"Mom," I said, my voice little more than a croak. "What're you doing?"

"Shut up," she told me and turned on the knife. The buzzing filled the room and went deep into my soul.

"Mom...." My heart rammed as urgency built but still, I could barely move on my own.

"Mommy's Baby." Mom looked down at Kristen. For that moment, I didn't exist. "Now Mommy's Baby don't need to grow up."

"Mom," I moaned. "No...."

The buzzing knife got closer to Kristen's pure white leg, just above the knee.

At least she's knocked out, I thought crazily. I looked over and noticed that, through quickly swelling eyes, she watched the electric knife with a look of such terror in her eyes that it made me push through the pain in my pelvis and wrestle against my ropes.

"Mom, *no!*" I screamed.

The electric blade broke skin and Kristen screamed. Blood squirted all over. I only noticed then that Mom had laid plastic out over everything.

The sound of the electric knife cutting through Kristen's

leg was the worst sound I've ever heard. Especially when it hit bone. It screeched as the motor caught and the knife stopped.

"Goddamn it." Mom pulled the knife out of Kristen's leg.

By now, Kristen had been out for a while but I howled, wondering if the neighbors heard me. They had to. I was screaming enough to fill the soundtracks of twenty horror movies.

Mom hit the handle of the knife with an open palm until it sputtered back to life. It soon buzzed with all the teeth-aching ferocity it had managed until it'd stalled. Without hesitation, Mom put the knife right back to the spot where it had frozen up and began pushing it down.

Kristen still didn't move.

She's in shock, I thought. *If she's lucky, she'll die.*

Once Mom was through Kristen's bone, finishing the rest of the leg was easy. She then went to work on the other one. My throat became so raw and voice so hoarse I stopped screaming. It was obvious to me by then that the neighbors either didn't hear me or didn't give a shit and the police weren't coming.

Once Kristen's other leg was detached, Mom turned the knife off and wiped the bloody sweat from her forehead. She looked at me—actually fucking looked at me like I was a co-conspirator—and said, "Wow. That was harder than I thought."

She put the knife down, took Kristen's detached legs, and put them in a Glad trash bag. After that, she opened the box of matches. She flicked one alight and started cauterizing the stubs of Kristen's legs.

The stench soon filled the small bedroom and finally pushed me over the threshold. I passed out.

Sometime later, Kristen's screams came from a great distance and I pushed myself toward them. Mom rushed into the room, trying to hush her by feeding her pills. I was about to say something or move but something told me not to. I closed my eyes and pretended to sleep. Mom calmed Kristen down as whatever narcotics she'd been given took effect. Soon, Kristen breathed slowly and evenly. I dared not peek. Mom's clothes rustled as she stood, took a few steps and stopped.

A chill rattled me. I felt her eyes on me. Felt the disgust and hatred radiating from them. She was insane. Even after I'd seen, heard, *smelled* what she'd done to Kristen's legs, a part of me still tried to rationalize her actions. But now it felt like the mist had finally lifted and I could see clearly. I don't know why, at that specific point, at that specific time it happened and not sooner... or later. I don't think I'll ever know. I don't care to be honest. I finally saw my mother for what she truly was: a monster. She was the Wicked Witch, the Big Bad Wolf, and every monster ever to grace the creature double feature. As I felt her eyes piercing me, as I forced my breathing to remain as calm and as evenly paced as Kristen's, I knew what thoughts ran through her mind. I was the weak link. I had to go.

"I'm sorry," Mom whispered and I couldn't help but go rigid, waiting for the fatal blow to fall. Then she left the bedroom.

I lay confused for several moments when a voice told me to get the hell out of there. But where would I go?

The police, stupid, a voice in my head said. *They'll take one look at you and know you're not fucking around.*

Though I remained submerged in intense pain and the grogginess and dizziness clung, I forced myself to move. My groin burned like hot coals had been shoved inside me and I bit the insides of my cheeks to stop from screaming and passing out. Once the worst of the stars and dizziness passed, I stood. The pain was no better and the room tilted as if on an ocean current. I held onto the wall, forced myself to take deep breaths, and held onto consciousness with everything I had. I staggered to the door.

Once there, I stopped and listened. Rustling came from Mom's bedroom across the miniscule hallway. She was going through one of her drawers, looking for something. In the pit of my stomach, I knew she wanted the gun.

The drawer closed and Mom began moving again. I peeked through the crack in the door and she stumbled into view, clutching the revolver in a quivering hand. Mom stopped, leaning against her doorway. I held my breath, certain she'd seen me. I wanted to turn away, screaming, but couldn't. The gun held me in a trance.

Then Mom turned and went back into her bedroom. I exhaled and looked around. I needed a weapon. But I was in a bedroom lived in by a seven-year-old girl and a seventeen-year-old girl, neither one athletic.

I heard her coming and decided surprise was as good as a weapon and grabbed my pillow. It was a heavy pillow stuffed with goose feathers.

At that moment, my bedroom door opened and Mom began to come in, holding her own pillow over the revolver. Before she was fully in the room, I smashed her in the face with the pillow. Pain tore through me. Mom was knocked a few steps back and the gun went off, spitting feathers from the new hole in her pillow.

I tackled her to the floor, ignoring my pain, and grabbed her gun hand. She screamed, calling me every name she could think of while I knocked the gun hand into the floor like I'd seen done in countless TV shows and movies. Her teeth sunk into the tender, white flesh of my forearm and I screamed as she tore a chunk out. She raised the pistol to my head and fired.

Everything stopped. I thought I'd died. I opened my eyes, though, and felt stinging on the back of my head and ringing in my ears. She'd missed.

She looked as stunned as I felt. I used this to my advantage and went for the gun again. This time I got a good hold on it and kneed her in the stomach with all my strength. She screamed as loud as my body did and her grip loosened enough for me to grab the gun.

Her hands shot up like claws and a thumb gouged my left eye as the other hand wrapped around my throat.

"You fucking bitch cunt whore you're dead fucking dead I shoulda killed you a long time ago—"

I pointed the gun in her direction and fired twice.

Her hands fell from my face and neck and I looked down. Two small holes were in her forehead. Blood, skull, and brains had sprayed the carpet beneath her head. I got up slowly, looking down at what I'd just done. She was dead. I'd killed her. It was over.

Over. They were going to put me away. I was going to live the rest of my life in jail.

I looked over at Kristen. Whatever pills Mom had given her

had knocked her out completely. I went over to her and put my trembling hand underneath her nose. She was still breathing. Mom hadn't given her an extra high dosage and she hadn't died.

I looked at the stumps Mom had given her. We were scarred, in more ways than we would ever show. I raised the gun and pointed it at Kristen. I tightened my grip.

I heard sirens approaching.

I looked at Kristen. She snored lightly.

I loved her. I didn't want her to suffer.

But, again, I couldn't do it.

Two police officers, a man and a woman, found me sitting on the floor between our beds, zoned out. The male cop suggested I was doped out of my mind and had tried to kill my family. The woman cop told him to get to the car and call for more help. Then she knelt in front of me and slowly removed the gun from my hands.

I held my breath, waiting for cold steel to close around my wrists and the Miranda rights recited on every cop show I'd ever seen to be read.

I looked up at the cop, a Hispanic woman in her mid-to-late thirties, black hair tied back, and deep brown eyes. These eyes spoke to me before she did. They knew, they *knew.*

"How long has she been hurting you two?" she asked.

"Since forever," I said, voice cracking. Then I blacked-out.

STORY NOTES

"THE GROWTH OF ALAN ASHLEY"

I didn't know when I wrote this story that Alan Ashley, a loser by all means, would give me a career.

I originally wrote the story in October 2002. I was deeply depressed and beginning to find signs of just how unhappy I was in my marriage, as well as unhappy with the way I seemed to be holding myself back from accomplishing my dreams. I seemed to spend more time thinking about writing than actually doing it. One night, my ex-wife and daughter were in bed and I was on the toilet when the Voice told me to attempt writing "the story of the man who lived in a fantasy world and sees it crashing down." I'd begun it once before, in 2001, but it had stalled in less than a page.

The catalyst for it this time was the guidelines for an anthology called *Vivisections 2*. I wanted a vivisection of this character without resorting to cutting him open. Funny enough, the supernatural element came out of nowhere and when I questioned it, the Voice again told me to keep going.

Not that "The Growth of Alan Ashley" was immediately successful. It was passed over for *Vivisections 2* (with a glowing rejection e-mail; strange enough, the anthology never came to be), *Weird Tales* (who only commented on the margins), *Talebones*, and *Flesh & Blood* (who I also believe said some very nice things about it). I wanted to send something to *Borderlands 5* and thought "Alan Ashley" was weird enough, so figured, *What the hell?*

When I got an e-mail from Tom and Elizabeth Monteleone in May 2003 telling me that the story was on their "maybe list," I almost shit myself. One month later I got the e-mail saying they wanted to buy it.

The story has gone on to do a lot for me. Not only in terms of my career but also because it broke down walls that had stood in my way and I found myself writing stories in a way I never had before. Hell, without this story, I don't think this book would exist.

"DRAWN IN"

During a rainstorm one night, I looked out the window of the apartment I was living in at the time and saw a small mattress lying in the vacant lot next door. It had a strange indentation in its center, as though someone had left a TV sitting on it. The next morning, it was gone. I wondered who would take it and why?

At the time, I was preparing to separate from my ex-wife. It was a tough time and my thoughts kept going to my daughter Courtney. I knew she'd be hurt by the coming separation, but I hoped it wouldn't be much.

"Drawn In" started as an answer to the question of who would take the strange mattress that seemed to appear from nowhere and ended up being a story about a daughter's forgiveness. Of course, the separation was the only real "bad thing" I did to her, and I needed a reason for Harry to be homeless, so I gave him many more monkeys on his back. His daughter showing up came from nowhere, I never intended for it to be about a father and his daughter but stories often write themselves, and this one was no exception.

"INQUISITOR, INC."

I think it was in 2000 when I had this really bad dream. In the dream, I walked into my parents' living room and my then-wife and mother were there. They stopped talking the moment I entered the living room and I knew they'd been talking about me. This happened in real life all the time and it pissed me off.

"What?" I asked.

"Nothing," they said.

In the nightmare, it *really* pissed me off, and I grabbed my wife and began hitting her, screaming, "I'll make you talk!"

I woke up horrified. I'm not a violent person, though my stories sometimes contain graphic violence. But the idea was somehow planted: a person who used violence to get answers. I know, not a big stretch. It's been happening for thousands of years. But what if the person only worked for the government by contract? What if he just went to the highest bidder and had been involved in many conspiracies and also non-government stuff? Who would do this? Hans Gerlach was born.

That's a concept, not a story. The story is how he considers his clients and the steps he goes through to appease his own conscience and what happens when he doesn't follow his own strict regimen. What happens when he realizes *he's been wrong*?

"Inquisitor, Inc." was born. I hope, like I did with "Mommy's Baby Don't Need to Grow Up," that this story is well-written enough to ease some of the nasty things that happens.

"YOU MAKE MY FLESH CRAWL"

"You Make My Flesh Crawl" is another unpublished story. This, like several other stories in this collection, has gone through several incarnations. The most recent takes out the tragic love story aspect I'd introduced in the previous version and makes it a pure love story.

Love has been an obsession for me in the past few years. I've always had a romantic streak, but I noticed as my marriage fell apart that my mind kept returning to love. What makes it work and not work and all the rest? I know; I'm not very original. It's all been done to death. Better people than I am have explored it in song, literature, and drama.

In the case of "You Make My Flesh Crawl," I took out all the clever tricks and the "E.C. horror comics ending," as Tom Monteleone called it when he rejected the previous version for *Borderlands 6*. Instead, I went the other way. I think the story is better for it.

"KILL -13-"

"KILL-13-" did not appear in the original lineup of *Catalysts*. In an attempt to get more subscribers to *Dark Discoveries*, James Beach put out a small, free anthology through Dark Discoveries Publications called *Darker Discoveries*. He asked if I wanted to submit something and this story had been simmering for a little while.

I began my career as an educator by substitute teaching, and then became a teaching assistant. During that year as a TA, 2006-2007, there was a student who creeped me out. He was... *void*. He didn't smile, he didn't speak, he was just there. The following year I became a teacher. In the years since, I've met several students who've scared me. They're just...off. You worry about them. Unfortunately, we live in an age where politicians and gun nuts would rather have children (and teachers) go through traumatizing ALiCE training than allow sensible gun laws. And some of them believe in the mythological Good Guy With A Gun. It wasn't cool in 2008 and it's even worse now.

This story is about all of that. Trying to deal with all these emotions and fears. In some ways, it's a story that I worry about. What if someone reads this as more autobiographical than it actually is? As a teacher, could I be in trouble for this story? This is an insane but true fear. I don't think Grant is a particularly likeable character, but I think there's a certain amount of empathy the reader feels toward him, which is why I decided to include this story in the collection.

"ICARUS FALLING"

"Icarus Falling" was my first published short story. It was written on an Olivetti manual typewriter in the summer of 1998, a few months after my daughter was born. Kelly took Courtney out for the day to visit relatives and I set the typewriter up on the coffee table and sat down to write a story that would meet the guidelines Greg F. Gifune had sent to me concerning a "science fiction terror" magazine he was starting up called *Burning*

Sky. I wrote the first draft that day in the sweltering heat and revised it on my electric Smith Corona. I didn't own a computer yet.

I submitted the story, which I'd intended to be sort of B movie-ish in terms of some of the strangeness in it, yet I also wanted it to explore some real human stuff. I was barely twenty-one when I wrote it and it shows. Greg sent it back, saying that if I perhaps added more atmosphere he may buy it. So I worked my ass off in one night figuring out atmosphere and revising the story and sent it back to him. He accepted it for *Burning Sky's* second issue, which was published in February 1999.

I revised the story for inclusion in *Catalysts* but it's still a story by a young writer. Nearly twenty-three years have passed but those years have brought with them a lot of stuff. As Indiana Jones said in *Raiders of the Lost Ark,* "It's not the years, it's the mileage." I still think it's an entertaining story and since the theme of this collection is beginnings, it's apropos to include it.

"BURNED OUT"

It was early 2002 and sirens drove up Coffin Avenue, the street where I lived with my ex-wife and daughter. I heard them stop about a block away. Outside, people came from everywhere to go check out what was going on. Many had this sort of gleeful look about them that something was happening to break up the dull monotony of life. It made me think of people who watch buildings burn, half in horror, half dazzled by the show. It made me think of the way the news showed houses burning, which is bad enough, but then reaction shots of its victims.

And it angered me.

I knew if *I* were in that situation, I wouldn't want people watching. Elliot Marshall, who has many of the same hang-ups I had when I wrote this (and sometimes still wrestle with), was a man living the American Dream until a few sparks in a closet changed his life.

"SNOW DAY"

Some people like this story, some don't. I like it. A lot. The initial version was written around 1995 or 1996 during a particularly bad winter in my freshman year of college. The characters were little boys, inspired a little by an incident in the UK where two little boys murdered a younger child. I wasn't pleased with the story and put it away.

In 1998, my daughter Courtney was born. One day in 2000, my mind turned to "Snow Day." The Voice, which I was beginning to learn to listen to more often, asked, *What if the boys were girls…? Since you have a little girl now….*

The new version of the story was written from scratch, using only the memory of the original. Its size was a problem and I held onto it until I found the Internet magazine *Ideomancer* and liked what they were doing. I'd submitted a story or two, I believe, before sending them "Snow Day." They bought it and it was online until the summer of 2006.

"Snow Day" is short and sweet, a problem some critics have said, the reason it's so good others have said. None of it matters to me. *I* like it. This version has been slightly revised. If you haven't read it yet, I hope you like it. If you *have* read it, well, I hope you'll reread it and enjoy it again.

"THE UMBRELLA PEOPLE"

Back when I was still married to my ex-wife, there was a time my parents would take me, my ex-wife, and my daughter out on Saturday nights to a small restaurant for dinner. Nothing fancy or special, but the food was okay. On one of those nights, it rained and my mother carried an umbrella. As we sat at our table, my mother said, "All right, don't let me forget my umbrella, people."

"Where are they?" I asked.

"Where are *what*?" my mother replied.

"Your Umbrella People."

There were chuckles and the night went on. For some

reason, though, the idea of Umbrella People stayed with me. And, as things sometimes do in my mind, it became sinister.

In March 2003, the United States, backed by Great Britain, invaded Iraq. I was against the whole thing and felt a total loss of control. Our society, which I have so much faith in, was divided by lies and going to *war*, something I hoped I'd never see in my lifetime. And it didn't look like one of the World Wars, where there was a definite cause, but more like Vietnam, where who knew what reasons we were there?

During this time, I was still working at the New Bedford bus station on weekends. I brought my notebook computer with me (I believe a large portion—if not all—of "Fun Gus the Tap Dance Man" was written there) and one morning I sat at the keyboard, typed

THE UMBRELLA PEOPLE

and began writing.

This was the first story I sent to James Beach for *Dark Discoveries*. He bought it very quickly. The rest is history.

"STRAY CATS"

"Stray Cats" is the second story I ever had published and one I worked quite hard on. It was originally written in 1998 as a first-person narrative. In early 2000, I went back, put it in third person and changed the ending. I sent it to Greg Gifune's *The Edge* and he rejected it with a marked-up manuscript and a long letter saying if I made some of the suggested changes, he may accept it. This happened around four times, if I recall correctly. Greg basically gave me a free fiction writing course that helped in many ways. I'm still thankful for his time and patience.

A lot happened in the few months we sent the story back-and-forth. In late May, I got married. In mid-June, I went into the hospital for emergency surgery (later on finding out how close I was to dying had I *not* gone to the hospital when I did). Not long afterward, the story came back with more changes. I did them and sent them off.

Greg finally accepted "Stray Cats" and it was my first appearance in *The Edge: Tales of Suspense,* and the second story Greg accepted from me. I am still very grateful for the faith and support he showed in my work, which is why I hope this recently rewritten version makes the story even better. It certainly brings it closer to my current standards. I wonder what another five years will bring....

"OLD NELLY'S HIGH PRICE"

This story was published on the *Naked Snake Online* webzine as "Old Nelly's Black Magic Closet." I don't think many of you read it. That sort of relieves me because, once it was posted, I saw a lot of things I didn't like. This story has a special spot in my heart. It was one of the first stories I wrote in which I really tried to explore relationships. Husband-wife, father-daughter, Black-White. Shit, there's even a touch of religion thrown in (surprisingly, enough, none of *my* religious beliefs found their way into it). Perhaps it's a little too much in places, in this revised version I hope I made things more subtle though I've never really been known for subtlety.

One of the major changes between this version and the story that was originally written (and appeared online) is Old Nelly Janks. Originally, she never appeared "onscreen." Jimmy and Arnold were cleaning out her apartment in the projects because she'd died. However, she kept coming back to me, trying to weasel her way into other stories. She just wasn't dead. So here she is, alive and well and doing her thing and the story is the same story and, as far as I'm concerned, it's better than it was. And *that's* what it's all about.

"SOMETHING IN THE PIPES"

This story was first written in 2000, only a month or two before I went in for surprise surgery. That surgery left me with a colostomy bag and a sense of mortality. A year later, another surgery took away the colostomy bag and I sold the story to a small press magazine. The magazine soon switched formats from a print zine to a webzine and then only lasted a short time. It was posted in January 2003.

I had trouble deciding whether or not to include this story in *Catalysts*. I'm not really fond of the characters but I like the mean sense of humor the story has.

At one point, I'd planned on doing a trilogy with Stuart and even wrote the follow-up, "Something Else in the Pipes." The third story was to have him in a secret government lab because they realized that he was, for some reason, a portal to other dimensions. He would meet someone else who had some issues and they'd fall in love and run away together. "Something Else…" never went beyond the first draft and the third story still exists only in concept.

Some things are better left alone.

"FUN GUS THE TAP DANCE MAN"

This story is a tough one for me. For starters, in terms of auto-biographical content, this story is full of it. When I began it in February or March 2003, I was a month or two into my big return to college, working at a bus station, and I had some marital issues. Those things all made it into the story on their own.

The initial drafts had a much different ending. When I decided what to do in regards with my own life and marriage, Ryan's choice also seemed obvious and the story's ending reflected it.

The title of the story was "Fun Gus the Tap Dance Man" from the beginning. My best friend, Toby Gray, never signs his e-mails *Toby* but instead with different things (often he'll sign them *tacos*). One day he signed an e-mail *Fun Gus the Hat Dance Guy*. Well, I didn't want a hat dance guy, but a tap dance guy was okay and a tap dance man sounded better phonetically and, well, I've always liked tap dancing.

This story was originally conceived as The Story I Would Send To *Borderlands 5*. The thing was, it wasn't finished soon enough for my liking, so I sent "The Growth of Alan Ashley" instead. I guess things worked out. This was the second story

I sent to James Beach for *Dark Discoveries* and it was the second story of mine that he bought.

"MOMMY'S BABY DON'T NEED TO GROW UP"

Until now, much to my chagrin, "Mommy's Baby Don't Need to Grow Up" has been unpublished. Part of the fault is mine; I like this story too much to send it just anywhere.

In 2000, I got sick and almost died. In the hospital after major surgery, I was on a morphine drip. After three days, I began hallucinating. At the time, I was also a stay-at-home Dad, caring for my then two-year-old. I used to like to play a little rough with her sometimes, rolling around, let her sit on my belly while I bounced her—that sort of thing. Because the surgery left me with a colostomy bag (which was removed in 2001), I knew I wouldn't be able to rough-house. And because I was out of it, I kept thinking how I'd miss out on her childhood. It was silly, but I wasn't in my right mind. So, jokingly (and also under the influence of morphine), the Voice said, *Well, chop her legs off and she'll* never *grow* up.

Har har.

But the story was born.

I think the reason the story means so much to me is because it's one that, from the very beginning, I've taken the greatest care in telling. I knew that the only way this story wouldn't become a sick sonofabitch would be if I wrote at the top of my form. I think I did then and have revised it several times in the seven years since. Just as Jack Ketchum's *The Girl Next Door* and Jerzy Kosinski's *The Painted Bird* are ultimately as good as they are because their writers worked damn hard to write at the top of their game, I did the same with this story.

I hope you like it. And if you don't, well....

COPYRIGHT INFO

ABOUT THE AUTHOR

Bill Gauthier is the author of *Catalysts, Alice on the Shelf,* and *Shadowed*. His work has appeared in magazines and anthologies including *Dark Discoveries* and the award-winning *Borderlands* anthologies. He lives in Southeastern Massachusetts with his wife and children. By day he teaches in a media-based technology program at a vocational-technical high school, where he helps teenagers find their voices and follow their dreams. By night, he writes dark stories, middle-grade space adventures, essays, blog posts, and generally skirts the edges of acceptability and rebellion.

BIBLIOGRAPHY

Alice on the Shelf
Catalysts
Echoes on the Pond
Shadowed

Curious about other Crossroad Press books?
Stop by our site:
http://store.crossroadpress.com
We offer quality writing
in digital, audio, and print formats.

www.ingramcontent.com/pod-product-compliance
Lightning Source LLC
Chambersburg PA
CBHW020644180626
46816CB00003B/1111